## PLAYING FOR KEEPS

"And behind door number 2, we have Allison.
Taa-daa!" Melissa walked over to a small recess
in the wall and slid open the door.

Inside, a young girl was tied on the floor. She
was in her mid-teens. Her body was a mass of
cuts, bruises, and cigarette burns. "Pain," Melissa snorted. "She'll get used to it."

Traveler growled and grabbed the black-haired
woman by her mane. He pulled her away from
the girl and tossed her behind him. He heard her
hit the wall with a thud. He pulled the whimpering young girl to her feet.

"Put her down," he heard Melissa slur from behind him. "She's mine." He turned around. Melissa held his crossbow in her sweaty hands.
"You can't come in here and just take our toys
away."

Coming soon

## TRAVELER #2
### by D. B. Drumm

For a tankful of gas and a few clips of ammo, he led a caravan of the damned all the way to **KINGDOM COME**.

And be sure to look for the other Dell action series

## HAWKER
### by Carl Ramm

America's deadliest vigilante, he lives outside the law—to battle the forces no law can touch.

## THE BLACK BERETS
### by Mike McCray

They learned their lethal skills on the secret battle-fields of Vietnam. Now, they're fighting for them-selves and not even the government can stop them.

## TRAVELER #1

# FIRST, YOU FIGHT

## D. B. Drumm

A DELL BOOK

Published by
Dell Publishing Co., Inc.
1 Dag Hammarskjold Plaza
New York, New York 10017

Dell ® TM 681510, Dell Publishing Co., Inc.

ISBN: 0-440-12551-0

Printed in the United States of America

First printing—June 1984

In memory of Harry Porter

# 1

The bodies, or what was left of them, lay smoldering in a ditch one hundred yards off the road.

The slender man with the black bandanna tied round his forehead stood, motionless, surveying the scene before him. His steel-blue eyes regarded the cadavers passively. The bodies were small, slender. Women, most likely. Children, perhaps. Either way, he was sure they had been brutalized before being butchered.

He had seen it happen enough to recognize the method simply by the way the limbs were positioned—frozen for eternity kicking, clawing; there was nothing kind in the ultimate surrender.

The smoke filled the air with the stench of charred flesh.

The stranger squinted into the sunbaked distance. There was no sign of a camp, no trace of vehicle tracks. That meant there was a city of some sort nearby—the people before him citizens who had strayed a little too far from the safety of the fortress for their own good.

The stranger ran a calloused hand over his chin.

The bodies were still belching smoke. The blood on the ground was still moist.

Whoever did this did it recently. If the killers had left the area, he was safe. If they were still around, then he had just strolled directly into a . . .

"Trap!" he hissed as a rifle cracked from somewhere behind him.

He dove headfirst into the dirt as the bullet whizzed by, slicing through the air inches from his left eye, leaving a crater in the earth by his head.

Flat on his stomach, only a few feet from the acrid victims, he was an easy target. He'd have to change that status fast. The stranger slithered effortlessly behind what appeared to be the foundation of a gutted house.

He had enough cover for a standoff.

He started to pull his Colt Commander from the holster beneath his right arm, hesitated, and dropped it back in the holster.

The slab-sided beauty was ramped, throated, and had a lovely National Match trigger, but it was empty. No wonder the Boy Scouts took my badges away, he thought.

He almost chuckled out loud as he slid the empty Colt back into its home. He was playing the Game again. As always, his life was at stake. And, as always, he found himself getting a bit weary of the whole routine.

A second round splintered against a concrete block near his shoulder. Bad shot, he noted.

He unsheathed his combat knife, gripping the black aluminum handle tightly. Crouching on his knees, he propelled himself forward. He tumbled across the length of the fractured foundation.

He held his breath.

The rifle remained silent.

The man in the black headband tensed. Someone was approaching him from the back of the house. He could *feel* it. That was one gift the army had given him free of charge: a nervous system so hyper, so shot-to-shit, that he could almost *sense* other people nearby.

He held the knife tightly in his left hand. He felt the stalker come closer. There was no doubt in his mind that he could take out his pursuer.

But if the man was a roadrat, then he'd only be one member of a mob. And if this stalker was sent to fetch him, then the other rats were surely waiting at the stranger's abandoned car.

He tightened his jaw and returned the knife to its sheath. He had a fifty-fifty chance of not only getting out of this alive but walking away with some much-needed ammunition as well.

Roadrats had a tendency not to kill their victims right off. Like alley cats on amphetamines, they got their jollies out of toying with their prey before they went about slaughtering. The stranger took a deep breath and hoped that his pursuer was a typical nomad. If the guy turned out to be a loner, the stranger could wind up with his inner organs as outer decorations in a matter of seconds.

"Well, look what I found me!" a guttural voice wheezed from over the stranger's shoulder. "Put your hands behind your head and turn around real slow."

The stranger did as he was told and slowly faced the roadrat. The rag-clad man before him cradled a badly battered M-16. If this guy ever ran out of tape, he'd be unarmed. It wasn't as impressive as the little AR-180 the stranger had tucked away in his van, but the magazine would come in handy. And anyway, you could trade anything these days. The roadrat was muscular, yet awkward in his movements. His face resembled half a pound of chopped steak, the entire left side composed of layers of flash-burn scars. A thin river of spit dribbled from between corrugated lips. The stranger guessed that this specimen had been caught too close to a major target during the last nuke-out.

"We're armed, eh?" the roadrat said, coughing. He extended a gnarled hand toward his captive and demanded the empty Colt. The stranger complied. For some reason the roadrat didn't take note of the knife strapped around the stranger's waist. Sloppy. Very sloppy.

"We already found your car," the pursuer snarled. "Hey! I got an idea. Let's go trash it!"

The stranger eyed the half-face. The roadrat obviously wasn't going to kill him . . . just yet. Hardcore baiting was in order first. The stranger relaxed slightly. His face must have betrayed his newfound sense of calm, for the scarred stalker took a sudden leap forward, striking the captive hard in the face with the butt of his rifle.

"I don't like you," half-face rasped. "I don't like you at all."

The stranger took the blow. He felt the blood trickle from the right side of his forehead. He did not flinch. He did not fall.

He nodded at the roadrat. "Well . . . there you go."

The two men glared at each other, both fully aware that the roadrat was under orders to capture and not to kill. Half-face snarled, impotent. "Come on. Move it."

The stranger marched toward his car, still parked on the roadside, the stalker holding the rifle securely at the small of his back. Sloppy. He could take this fool anytime.

As the pair moved away from the bombed-out foundation, a pack of wild dogs materialized from the shadowy debris and pounced upon the smoldering corpses. The stranger left the murder site with the sounds of growling and snapping jaws lingering in his ears.

Three rifle-toting marauders awaited his arrival at his van. Two were emaciated scarecrows. They wore the blank expressions of plague victims. The third stalker was a portly, bearded giant, six feet four, wearing a raincoat big enough to serve as a circus tent. One didn't have to be a military genius to figure out who the leader of this hunting party was.

"Colonel," half-face wheezed, "look what I found hiding out with our harem."

The stranger involuntarily sneered at the mention of military rank.

The fat man noticed it. He puffed up his chest to imposing proportions and waddled toward his captive.

"What're you hunting, mister? Boys? Girls? Is that your story? You trying to get a little something to keep you warm on a cold night?"

The colonel grinned, exposing teeth that could have served as a harmonica ad. "Well, we beat you to it! We did them. We did them all to death. Got 'em a little too hot, though. Maybe we'll warm your butt up, too, before we're done."

The stranger stared at the colonel placidly. He obviously wasn't in the mood for small talk.

This man mountain wanted some satisfaction from his prisoner and was obviously puzzled by his prisoner's lack of concern. "Hmmm. We got ourselves a thinking man, here." Sweat was beginning to form on his furrowed brow. "Strong silent type, huh?"

The colonel's face grew flushed. He began stroking his beard relentlessly. "You think you're special because you have a shiny car? Well, you don't seem too damn special to me, mister driver. You ain't big enough or strong enough to take any of us, and that sissy bandanna round your head makes you look like you might *want* us to warm your butt a bit."

The stranger offered a barely perceptible smile by way of reply.

This was not what the colonel wanted. He wanted the man to beg before he killed him. This was his game, and this stranger was ruining it. The colonel began to shake as he eyed his prey. "Well. Army pants. Army shoes. You a grunt? I bet that's it. You're a grunt. Well, listen up. The army's not worth shit anymore. You know what we do to grunts here?"

The stranger remained silent.

"We skin 'em and eat 'em!" half-face cackled from behind.

"Shut up, Harlan," the colonel barked.

The two rat zombies stood, immobile, next to the stranger's van, staring blindly into space.

11

"What's your name?" the colonel suddenly demanded. "You got a name?"

"They call me Traveler."

"Traveler?" the fat man fumed. "What kind of a name is that?"

"Mine."

"And what is it you do, Mister Traveler?"

"I move."

The colonel pulled back a fist as if to strike the stranger. A look in Traveler's eyes caused him to think better of it. The fat man took his upraised hand and scratched his beard instead.

"A real mystery man we got here, Harlan. Hey, Traveler. I heard a couple of stories about a mercenary who wanders around these parts. He hires himself out for scutwork. Could that be you?"

"Could be."

"Well, you know what we do with mercenaries around here?"

Before the colonel could elaborate, half-face offered a breathless reply. "We skin 'em and eat 'em!"

Traveler stared at the colonel. "Interesting diet you boys have."

Traveler offered the fat man a boyish smile. He spoke softly, yet firmly. "Now, why don't you put down your weapons and walk away. We'll call it even."

Traveler's voice had been no more than a whisper. The colonel reacted as if he had heard a grenade go off. Clearly, the burly man was dumbfounded. Flecks of white danced out of his mouth as he tried to figure whether to laugh or lie down and wait for this fool to go away. "Are you crazy? Hey! Mister Traveler. Look around you. There are four of us and one of you. We have guns. You got nothing."

Traveler did not smile. He did not blink. "Put down the guns and we'll call it even."

"You're some sick dude," the colonel exclaimed, shaking his head incredulously. "Hey. You carrying food or guns inside that van of yours?"

He pointed to the mini-van next to the two zombies.

Traveler had a Heckler and Koch HK91 heavy assault rifle, a Remington 870 Brushmaster 12-gauge, an Armalite AR-180 light assault rifle, and enough C-rats stashed inside to keep moving. He nodded at the colonel. "Yup."

"You got balls, travelin' man, but no smarts. You're on the outside of that car, and your weapons are all on the inside. Looks to me like you're stuck. And there you stand givin' *me* orders. You don't give orders around here. You take 'em. You're my prisoner, shithead. Got that?"

Traveler sighed. He was growing tired of the Game. Why was it no one would just leave him alone?

A sudden gust of wind blew a thin veil of dust over his face. He blinked the soot out of his eyes. No telling what was in that grit. Fallout. The remains of families, cities, countries—entire civilizations blasted into pulverized particles. All because of idiots. Traveler shook these thoughts from his mind and faced the fat roadrat.

"The offer still stands," he said flatly.

The colonel motioned to the two zombies. "Let's see what's inside the van. Heard, you take the back. Wenders, pull everything out of the front seat."

"Last chance," Traveler offered.

The colonel bounced slowly up and down on the balls of his feet, defying several laws of gravity, and regarded his captive with a loathsome grin. "I'm gonna watch when them dogs get to you, merce. And I'm gonna enjoy seein' them tear that smartass tongue right out of your head."

The zombie Wenders opened the door on the driver's side of the van and stuck his head inside. His body jerked once. He emitted a gurgling cry.

"What's that?" the colonel demanded.

Wenders muttered something unintelligible a second time as he slowly began pulling himself out of the front seat.

"What's that, Wenders? I can't understand what you're saying!"

"He says he can't complete his mission, Colonel," Traveler explained. "He's just set off a crossbow trip wire."

Wenders body tumbled out of the car, an eight-inch arrow embedded in his neck.

A horrible scream emerged from the back of the van. The colonel's face went ashen. Traveler offered a lopsided smile. "And *that* will be the big stick."

Before the colonel had time to react, Traveler pulled his Gerber survival knife and leaped forward, slashing the colonel once across his right arm. The fat man loosened his grip on his M-16 for a split second. Traveler yanked the weapon from the man, spun around, and kicked the burly roadrat forward toward a paralyzed Harlan, still clutching his battered gun like a talisman.

Traveler trained the rifle on the two roadrats. The colonel landed on his knees, seething. Holding his injured arm with a bloodied hand, he bellowed at halfface. "Kill him, Harlan! Kill him!"

Traveler stared at the twitching half-face. "You can still walk away from this."

"Kill him!" the colonel whined. "Kill him!"

Half-face hesitated. He took a step back. The colonel continued screeching orders. Half-face nodded and moved the rifle toward Traveler.

Traveler set his jaw and fingered the trigger on the rifle. The colonel may not have taken care of his troops, but his gun was in fine shape. Within seconds, the insides of both half-face and the colonel were splattered on the dusty macadam roadway by a stream of jacketed .223 slugs.

"Well, there you go," Traveler muttered, staring at the carnage. Some people were just too stupid for words. He picked up the dead roadrats' guns, retrieved his Colt, and walked back to the van. He tossed the two new rifles in the back. He could always trade them for food or ammo or gasoline. Pulling the arrow out of Wenders's neck, he snatched the third rifle.

By the time he began prying Heard off the back of his van, the packdogs were already feasting on the colonel.

Traveler glanced at the scrawny canines as they ripped and tore at the still-warm flesh. Damn. Once upon a time he'd even kept one of those creatures as a housepet. Before the Last War, of course. A sudden picture of a house, of Roberta and Kiel Junior flashed through his mind.

It dissipated as a wave of nausea swept through his body. He shouldn't have played the Game with four men. He knew it. Even though he was in one piece physically, his nerves were fragmented. He just couldn't take being around a lot of people. On really bad days four could be a real crowd. Traveler banged his fist against the side of the van. Once. Twice. Three times. The nausea subsided.

Traveler heaved a sigh and dumped the live rounds into a butt-pack he kept next to the front seat of the van. He quickly loaded his light assault rifle and some spare clips. He also loaded up the Colt, even jacking a round into the chamber. The next time he had to play the Game, he'd do it well armed. He started up the car and cruised to the top of the hill before him.

He braked suddenly, staring in awe at the seeming mirage below. At the bottom of the hill, not five hundred yards away, stood a town. An actual goddamn town. With green trees. And lights. And old-fashioned, ivy-covered buildings that hadn't been ravaged by man or machine.

Gazing at the incredibly tranquil scene, Traveler had a hard time remembering that the Last War had ever happened. Here before him was a remnant of a time past. A time that had occurred before radiation, before MX, before the plagues and the packdogs and the roadrats and the mutants.

A time when Traveler still had a name.

Reality ripped up the dream as Traveler became aware of the barbed wire and bunkers lining the outskirts of the small city. Welcome back to the nightmare.

Traveler shrugged. Still, for an armed fortress, the place was truly beautiful.

A sudden chill caused the hairs on the back of his neck to rise. He shuddered to think what his nerves would go through if he ever had to spend more than five minutes in a town that large, an area populated by two or three thousand people. He'd probably come apart at the seams.

His face grew flushed. He slammed a fist down on the dashboard. He was a loner. He didn't need anyone else. He *couldn't* need anyone else. Enraged at what the army had done to him and the world had done to itself, Traveler shifted the car into reverse and executed a squealing K-turn in the middle of the road.

He sped off in the opposite direction, a solitary mercenary on the move. The city disappeared over the hill in his rearview mirror. Fuck if he'd ever go near a hick burg like that anyway.

Without warning, a bullet slammed off the van's shatterproof windshield.

Traveler blinked and gaped at the road stretching northward. One hundred roadrats, heavily armed, on foot, on horseback, and on the back of a couple of flatbed trucks were charging toward him.

Traveler stood on the gas and hung a deranged bootleg turn, speeding back toward the lush cityscape.

Then again, maybe a quick stop in a quiet town might be just what the doctor ordered.

# 2

The projectile was black and tear-shaped, roaring louder and louder as it accelerated.

The two men standing guard in the bunker behind the barbed wire barricade could not believe their eyes.

"It's a car!" the taller of the two sentries cried. "And the fool's heading right for us!"

"Get the lead out, shithead!" his companion hissed as he slapped a belt of 7.92 mm into the M-60 they were supposed to use to protect the town from things like this.

In the mini-van, Traveler hit the accelerator as he approached the blockade. There was no way he could simply plow through the mass of wire, wood, and metal without damaging the Meat Wagon pretty badly. With the roadrats on his tail, however, there was no way he was simply going to turn around and head back down the road.

If he couldn't go through the barricade, maybe he could go over it. He took note of a small dirt mound— maybe an old bunker—off the side of the road. Swerving off the concrete and into the dirt, he stood on the gas pedal, watching his speedometer all the while.

The Meat Wagon hit the mound at around eighty and sailed into the air. Traveler smiled to himself as he watched the barricade and the trembling guards who had hit the dirt pass beneath his wheels. Hell. He had cleared the barbed wire with at least an inch to spare. No sweat.

The car smashed onto the town's main street with a scream of rubber. Traveler braked hard, sending the vehicle into a violent, fishtailing slide. The auto came to rest in the middle of a deserted, decidedly ivy-league-town street. He glanced in the rearview mirror. The guards were still flat on their stomachs and out of sight. There was no sign of the pursuing roadrats.

Traveler stepped out of the Meat Wagon. He set his trip wires, eased the door shut, and pressed the lock with his thumb, activating the trip-wire booby traps. He stood next to the car and surveyed the town before him.

It was in perfect condition. There were none of the signs usually associated with World War III's aftermath. It was as if the entire city had been covered by some sort of protective bubble during the nuke-out.

Unscathed houses and shops stretched for blocks and blocks, all quaint, two- and three-story structures. A block to Traveler's right a white church with a steeple stood serenely. Picket fences lined the homes on the side streets. An American flag flapped in the breeze, high atop a flagpole in front of a building that must have been the city hall. In the distance, a small but imposing college campus stood; a mixture of red brick and green foliage.

It was all-American. Apple pie. Andy Hardy.

Unreal.

Traveler stiffened slightly, catching the presence of two, maybe three, angry life-forms approaching him from behind. He turned very slowly and faced three grizzled young men. They wore national guard uniforms.

Traveler almost burst out laughing. That's just what he needed for comic relief. Guardsmen! Weekend warriors, heavily armed and lightly IQ'd. They carried all the right toys, but in the aftermath of the Great Disaster, proved to be less than worthless when it came to police actions. The country had fallen apart after the war, and the Guard had shattered right along with it.

Traveler didn't like people in general.

He didn't like national guardsmen in particular.

"Yo, speed-o," said the ranking rifleman, a corporal, in a vague attempt at sarcasm, "what's your problem?"

Traveler sighed. Another round of the Game was in the offing unless he could avoid it. "No problem."

"No problem?" the guardsman exclaimed for the benefit of his amused peers. "You crash the town's perimeter, invade the city, and park your car in a towaway zone, and you tell me there's no problem?"

"Okay, I'll move the car," Traveler said, easing open the door on the driver's side.

"Back away from the car," the lead guardsman said. Traveler eased the door closed. The guardsmen slowly approached him. "Nice wheels. Wankel engine, I bet. Four-wheel drive. Definitely nice wheels."

The guardsman took his rifle and slammed it onto the hood of the Meat Wagon, causing a small dent. "Must be hot stuff to have a car of your own, huh?"

Traveler said nothing. Very casually, he fingered a metal-studded wristband on his right arm.

"Bet you got the car booby-trapped, too." The guardsman grinned, slamming the butt of his rifle into the driver's door. Another dent.

"Suppose we see if we can neutralize this invading auto." The guardsman nodded to his grinning friends as he pulled the loading lever of his M-16.

In an almost imperceptible movement, Traveler pulled a four-pronged shurikan from his wristband and let it fly with a flick of his left hand. The metal star caught the lead loudmouth in the forehead, making a small, crunching noise. The man let out a yell as the blood spurted down his face. He collapsed, writhing, in front of the car.

Before the other two guardsmen could fire, Traveler hurled two more shurikans their way, catching one man in the throat, the other neatly between the eyes.

19

Traveler stepped over the body of the lead guardsman and surveyed the damage to his car. "Sure hope someone does bodywork in this town," he muttered.

He opened the front door and pulled out a small crossbow. The bow was lightweight but rugged, made of polypropylene with a graphite fiber bow and possessing a thumb-hole pistol grip. The mini-bow looked a little bit like a sawed-off shotgun, had a 130-pound draw, fired eight-inch arrows, and would probably come in very handy until Traveler stocked a little more ammunition. Besides, it wouldn't do to disturb the peace in this town. Judging by his reception, this town might prove less tranquil than its appearance would indicate. Traveler closed the door of the Meat Wagon, setting the trip wires, and strolled across the street to a restaurant-bar bearing the name Leone's.

Traveler didn't know what the method of barter was hereabouts, but he figured he could trade something or other for a meal and a drink.

He entered the establishment, blinking his eyes while attempting to adjust to the dim lighting. The place was a travesty of chic normalcy. Potted ferns hung from the ceiling. Earth-colored stained-glass windows reflected the sunlight on the room's few patrons in jagged patterns. A full bar stood off to the side of the room. A large black man stood behind the counter. Traveler approached the bar.

"You the owner of this place?"

"Do I look like my name is Leone?" The bartender smirked. Traveler said nothing. The bartender shrugged. "Let's just say I run the place."

"You stocked?"

The barkeep, a sad-eyed man in his fifties, offered a lopsided grin. "Yeah. Not too much business anymore."

"You take American dollars?"

"Dollars. Rations. Canned food. Poultry. You name it. I'll take it. For you, though, it'll be on the house."

"Thanks. Give me a shooter, then."

The barkeep poured a shot of golden tequila into a glass and shoved it Traveler's way. Traveler downed the drink. His body trembled slightly. The alcohol would keep his nerves in check somewhat. He felt a wave of claustrophobia surge up deep within him. He ordered another shot. The barkeep poured.

"Why the generosity?" Traveler asked.

"Lease I can do for a dead man." The barkeep shrugged.

Traveler looked at him quizzically. The man began to explain. "You just killed three of Aikers's men. He's not going to like that very much."

"Maybe he'll get over it."

The barkeep caught sight of the dog tags around Traveler's neck. "Army." He nodded. "I figured as much."

Traveler motioned for another drink; he had to keep his composure. The bartender didn't notice the sweat on Traveler's upper lip. He continued to chat. "Terrance Bellows is the name. Formerly Sergeant Terrance Bellows. Did a couple of tours of Nam and Nicaragua. Honorably discharged with more metal in my back than most hardware stores keep in stock."

Traveler downed the shot. Bellows scrutinized him carefully. "You have a name?"

"Had one. I gave it up."

"I hear you, man. Where were you stationed?"

"El Hiagura."

"No shit!"

"Total shit."

Bellows squinted his hound-dog eyes until they resembled hyphens. "Wait a minute. Wait a minute. El Hiagura. That was a real hot spot, man. Pro-commie government. Pro-Yank guerrillas. There were only five American military men down there, right? Part of a UN peace-keeping force. You one of them?"

"You serve any food here?"

"Yeah. You like your canned meat cold or hot?"

"Just give me the can and a spoon."

"Yeah," Bellows said, producing a battered tin. "The five of you. The President sent his right-hand man, Captain Vallone, to head that team. What a shit. El Hiaguran government said you were aiding the guerrillas. Vallone got out. Yeah. I remember the headlines. The other four bastards got it with neurotoxins. First time that shit was ever used in combat. Can't count on the Geneva Convention if you don't call it a war. Poor bastards. Twisted. I remember that. Poor bastards. You one of those guys?"

Traveler pulled the spoon out of his mouth. "This tastes like cat food!"

"Naaah. Dog food. Alpo. 1986. Vintage year. Yeah, I figured you for regular army. You're no guardsman. Those guys are psychos, man. Undisciplined shitheels. This town was doing okay until they arrived. Until they got here and Milland's crew got here."

Traveler took another swallow. It didn't taste so bad if you didn't think about it. Traveler was good at not thinking about things. "Is there a place I could bunk?"

"There's a Holiday Inn down the block." Bellows grinned. "They don't care if you don't have a reservation."

Traveler motioned for another shot. He had to go someplace to shut down soon. His body was beginning to react. Every noise in the bar seemed to echo like thunder in his mind. Every small movement Bellows made seemed threatening. The smell from the meat was beginning to make him sick. He swallowed the liquor. He had to keep a lid on things. He'd shower. He'd sleep. He'd see if he could trade a couple of guns for some extra ammunition and gasoline and then get the hell out of town.

"Where am I, anyhow?" he asked.

"Tendran, Utah. Near the Nevada border. About four hundred miles from where Salt Lake City used to be."

"Used to be?"

"Yeah. Russians took out Salt Lake City in the second wave. You probably passed it and just didn't notice it. It's that big flat spot that glows in the dark." Bellows snorted, his nostrils flailing. "That was a joke."

"I'll laugh later."

Traveler turned to leave the restaurant. A policeman, gun drawn, stood in the doorway. "That your car out front?"

"Yeah."

"You're parked in a towaway zone."

Traveler sighed. "Why don't you just ticket me and then arrest those three guardsmen loitering outside in the street."

The officer, a sturdy but confused fellow, pondered that last remark. As he did so, three men carrying rifles entered the restaurant. Traveler had the feeling he had just strolled into an armed camp. "We'll take care of this, Tommy."

The policeman turned, and seeing the three very determined citizens framed in the doorway, backed off gracefully.

"I'm Moon," the bald-headed citizen in the fore-ground announced. "I work for Mr. Milland."

Traveler refrained from applauding.

"Mr. Milland would like to see you."

"Well, here I am."

"Mr. Milland would like to talk to you about those guardsmen outside."

"They're dead. What more is there to say?"

"Mr. Milland doesn't like guardsmen, either. He'd like to talk to you about a job."

Traveler stared at the bald man with the gun. "Suppose I don't want a job?"

"Then we'd like to talk to you about your funeral."

Traveler glanced at Bellows. The barkeep only shrugged. Traveler sighed and walked toward the three men. "Come to think of it, I guess I could use a bit of employment."

The foursome stepped out into the sunlight, the three men surrounding Traveler. The police officer was dragging the dead guardsmen onto the sidewalk.

"Excuse me for a minute," Traveler said, breaking away from the group before they could react. Traveler bent over the slain men and removed the pointed metal stars from their bodies. Wiping the blood off on his trousers, he replaced the shurikans in his wristband.

"These things are hard to come by," Traveler explained.

Moon was not impressed. He motioned for Traveler to keep walking.

# 3

Traveler sat in the mahogany-trimmed study and blinked into the sunlight filtering in through the window blinds. Small storms of dust whirled and swirled in the thin shards of light. The dust particles floated like feathers. Like snowflakes. Like shrapnel. For a split second he was once again sprawled on the jungle floor of a country he didn't know about, didn't care about, and wished to God he had never heard about.

He blinked again.

He found himself back, seated before a large, wooden desk.

Traveler had a problem with time.

He tended to drift, occasionally, from present to past, from past to future. It didn't seem to matter much to him anymore. One time was as good as the next.

It had been fifteen years since time became meaningless. Fifteen years since the world had gone to shit. In 1989 the unthinkable became the thinkable. Nightmares had become reality.

World War III blossomed all around the globe.

Traveler had been in a V.A. hospital at the time, trying desperately to keep his insides from rolling out his ears. No one had expected the war to happen. It was just one of those unexpected things, like stubbing your toe on a table in your own home after passing it safely on countless other occasions.

Traveler blinked. 1989.

The president of the United States at the time was one Andrew Frayling, a yahoo in his fifties. He had actually started out as a cowboy TV star. No kidding. What he really was was a smooth voice and nice complexion with a snake pit set of advisers who seemed intent on the Republic turning a profit. Whether there was anyone other than themselves and their cronies left to share it seemed to matter little to them.

Regardless of the hows and whys, Frayling had been at the helm in '89. More frightening than that fact was that, apparently, he still thought of himself as a six-gun star. He kept everybody and everything jumping for his three years in office, trying to take America's mind off inflation and unemployment. He succeeded in plunging the country into a new Cold War, which was very good for business. Then one day, somehow, somebody took him seriously and the world ended.

The end of the world started with a milk run. Everybody ran them. Every Monday or every Friday—depending on what color your flag was—planes went up and played chicken with the opposition's radar. You found out what they had, and they saw that you were still in the Game. This time, though, the plane, a U.S. spotter, went in a little too close and shots were fired. First, the spotter went down, and then the Russians got burned by the spotter's high cover.

The Russians retaliated . . . in a big way. What had been a military exercise in East Germany became a hot, hard probe at NATO defenses. The U.S. rattled its Pershings, and the Sovs went all the way. Pushed the big red one. Maybe they had been watching Frayling's movies in Moscow.

Frayling had been in too many of those movies, and he played his part like a true western hero. He launched everything America had. Contrary to some stories, the mushrooms were not red, white, and blue. They were just bloody. When the Soviets saw that their first strike would hit nothing but empty silos and deserted harbors, they launched a second salvo aimed at the most populous cities in the U.S.A.

It was bigger and better than any Fourth of July.

World War III was a draw. There were no winners. Only losers. The two great superpowers were in ruins as was most of the rest of the world. The various border skirmishes that had been held in check for decades because of the two countries' political presence erupted. Without any global police action, the third world gang had a field day; engaging in conventional, nuclear, and germ warfare. Pakistan attacked India. Iraq took on Iran. Brazil invaded Argentina. In Europe, British and Irish forces went at it hand to hand while, on the continent, the Western and Eastern blocs nearly destroyed each other.

Within seven days an entire world had been ripped apart.

By the time Traveler stumbled out of the hospital, allegedly a whole man, there was no home to flee to. No house. No family. No town. Hell, half of the fucking state had disappeared.

So, he "borrowed" a car from one of the hospital honchos. Eventually, he customized it. He renamed it the Meat Wagon, both in honor of his past wartime experiences and his present status, and started to travel.

For the past decade and a half he had done whatever necessary to stay alive. And, lately, staying alive wasn't meaning as much to him as it used to. He no longer feared death. Some days he even longed for it. In Traveler's world the survivors of the last war envied the casualties. Every day was like a stroll through Hades.

"So this is our assassin, eh?"

Traveler blinked.

The jungle disappeared. The hospital vaporized. The cadavers crumbled; the radioactive hot spots faded away.

He was sitting directly across from a tall, gaunt man whose high forehead was surrounded by tufts of white

27

hair. The man wore a three-piece suit and went out of his way to project a sense of predatory calm. Had this been fifteen years ago, Traveler would have assumed the fellow to be a captain of industry, a congressman, or perhaps, a high-class pimp.

"I am Franklin Milland," the gentleman announced.

"I am less than thrilled," Traveler replied.

Milland's eyes were the color of old steel, gray, flecked with bits of red. His lips were thin and colorless. When he smiled, it reminded Traveler of a crocodile's grin. It was not the sincerest sight in the world.

With a remarkable show of agility for a man pushing sixty, Milland lurched over the desk and yanked the dog tags from around Traveler's neck. Traveler didn't flinch. Milland stared at the dog tags. "I should have guessed." He chuckled. "No name, just a blood type."

Traveler shrugged. "Art imitates life."

Milland tossed the dog tags back at the mercenary. Traveler caught them effortlessly with a quick move of his left hand. Milland settled back into his chair, folding his hands on the desk top.

"My dear sir. From your appearance and your performance, I gather you are a mercenary, a soldier of fortune. Am I correct?"

Traveler stared impassively.

Milland took no notice. "Whatever. I have no idea what has brought you to our little town, but I feel that we can both benefit if we work together."

Milland pursed his lips, awaiting a reply. Getting none, he continued. "Before the war, I was a very rich man. In a sense, I am still a very rich man. I am rich because I am clever. I am not a humanist. I am not sentimental. I am sorry there was a war, but that's done with. I have survived. I have been allowed to live to pursue my interests. There is only one thing that I am interested in, and that is power—the power to survive a little longer and a little more comfortably."

Noting Traveler's lack of enthusiasm, Milland arched

a gray eyebrow and smiled slightly. "Am I going too fast for you?"

"Hardly."

"Excellent. As you've probably noted, this town is quite remarkable in its own little way. Before the war it was a college community—lots of smart, healthy people. When the bombs dropped, the people took care of business. They have managed to keep the town running smoothly over the years.

"Unfortunately, the war happened during Christmas vacation. Had the entire student and faculty population been present during the aftermath, they probably could have transformed this town into a veritable Eden. As it is, it's quite an efficient ecosystem. It has electricity, running water, and most of the conveniences one associates with prewar life.

"Now. While this town was working to keep up the facade of postnuclear normalcy, I was quietly hiring an effective army of well-skilled mercenaries. Why? Quite simply . . . to be able to find towns like this one and take them over. In the past five years I have successfully occupied sixteen small cities. It's a very old game—I protect them from roadrats and other deadly vermin . . . like my men.

"This will be my capital. Capital of my country or kingdom, if you prefer feudal terminology. From this town, I will rule."

Traveler cleared his throat and spat on the floor.

"I hope that wasn't an editorial comment," Milland said. "At any rate, eventually I intend to rebuild and conquer this entire state. Once this state is solidified, I want to spread my power base to other states. Perhaps, someday, I will rule the entire country. Who knows? In America, dreams come true, correct? Unfortunately, certain problems have arisen which threaten my plan."

Traveler blinked. The jungle appeared and disappeared. He had to get some sleep and soon. "Such as?"

"Short range . . . we have the presence of Captain

29

Zeke Aikers and his rather rambunctious national guard goons. They established a base in this town just about the same time I arrived. Unfortunately, our forces are approximately equal. I can't bring men in from the other towns because we're stretched impossibly thin as it is. This has resulted in a standoff. Neither one of us can win, so we both bide our time."

"What do the citizens of the town do while you folks . . . bide your time?" Traveler inquired.

"Oh, fuck the people. We're talking power here."

"Sorry."

"My biggest problem, however, is President Frayling."

Traveler couldn't believe his ears. "Frayling is still alive?"

"Oh, very much so. Alive and well and attempting to rebuild the country from a new White House in Nevada. Vegas, I believe. He has his loyal troops galloping through the country, forcing towns and cities into submission. They are out to reunite the states come hell or high water with Sheriff, excuse me, President Frayling calling the shots. It's a sort of nouveau manifest destiny motif that, while quaint, is quite troublesome to me in light of my own political aspirations."

"I can imagine."

Moon and his two cronies walked into the room as if on cue. Traveler figured they had been listening to the entire spiel from outside the door. Milland became very serious. "I am always looking for new merces for my team. I know I can use you. I want this town. I will have it. With your . . . dexterity on my side, I believe I can hasten the process."

"I'm only one man."

"But you have survived all these years by yourself . . . out there," Milland said, motioning to the window. "It takes quite a man to do that."

"Survival is easy. Living isn't."

Milland shook his head, dismissing the comment. "I'm not a philosopher. Bottom line, sir. There's a shipment of guns passing through this area soon. Frayling's troops, his Glory Boys, are bringing them back to Nevada. I need those guns to defeat Aikers, to take over this town, and to move on from here."

Traveler stared at Milland. Guns. Ammunition. That would explain the large number of roadrats nearby. Every jerk in whatever state this is must know about the shipment.

"Where do I fit in?" Traveler asked.

"I want you to take a few of my men and find the shipment. Scout around for me out there. I know you can do it. You've survived out there. You know the territory."

"What's in it for me?"

"What do you need? Ammunition? Supplies? You name it."

Traveler stood up. "I will, too."

Milland leaned back in his chair. "You accept my offer?"

Traveler slowly turned to face the doorway. Moon's two men had their rifles trained on his back. "Do I have a choice?"

"Not really."

"I'll need gasoline for my car."

"No problem. There are two service stations in town with full tanks. I control one. You'll be staying at the Holiday Inn?"

"Yeah," Traveler said, nodding, "even though I hate the decor."

Traveler headed for the door, pushing his way past Moon and his men. Milland called after him. "You never told me your name."

Traveler walked down a flight of stairs leading to the ground floor. "I know," he replied.

Traveler walked out of the building and stepped into the afternoon sun. He hated men like Milland. It was people like that who had led the world into the last war—fat cats who had forgotten that human beings were more than mere statistics or fighting machines or dots on a map.

The thought of working for Milland sickened him. The thought of being shot in the back by one of Milland's men, however, made him feel even worse. So, that was that.

Before he could take two steps into the street, Traveler was grabbed from behind. He was spun around roughly. He found himself eyeballing two very disturbed national guardsmen. "Captain Aikers wants to see you," said a man with no teeth.

Traveler should have smelled this one coming. He shrugged and allowed himself to be shoved down the opposite direction of main street. Some days you ate the bear, and some days the bear ate you.

# 4

Captain Zeke Aikers was short, stocky, and exceedingly oily. His skin possessed the sort of sheen usually associated with overcooked sausage. His uniform was seemingly perplexed by the contours of the man's body with the buttons of his shirt apparently seeking to find a way into low earth orbit. He had a pug nose and heavy jowls and was one of those balding types who combed his one lone strand of black hair every which way in a vain attempt to cover the top of his head. The areas of his face that weren't creased were pockmarked. Aikers would never be a poster boy.

Despite his substandard looks, however, he was having a good time hammering his ham-sized fists into Traveler's midsection while two of his uniformed uglies held Traveler's arms.

Traveler sagged under the repeated blows, feeling every muscle in his abdomen contract and expand. Pain. He was used to pain.

This was nothing compared to '89.

Orwell, Margolin, Hill, and Traveler had been out on a routine assignment when the great pain had struck. Captain Vallone had set them up. He had never figured out why.

"The area is safe," Vallone had told them. "No sign of government troops."

They really weren't supposed to be conducting mili-

33

tary maneuvers in El Hiagura in the first place. But these weren't ordinary maneuvers, just as these four men were nothing like ordinary soldiers. Their cover said that they were members of a peace-keeping mission. In reality, they were four boys from the Blue Light Brigade—men who worked in the Long Range Reconnaissance Patrols and did the other dirty jobs in the dirty little wars around the world—and now they were in El Hiagura to provide covert assistance and training to pro-American guerrillas trying to overthrow the pro-Communist government. These men were soldiers like missiles are bullets. But even the best can be destroyed when someone introduces new rules.

The four of them had walked straight into an ambush that day in the jungle. The Hiaguran troops had a new toy, and they were just looking for someone to play.

Neurotoxins.

Although the United Nations frowned on such weapons and the Geneva Convention forbade them—who even remembers who signed the Charter or the Convention rules anymore? So, Hill, Orwell, Margolin, and a man who later called himself Traveler had the honor of becoming the first neural combat guinea pigs. The funny thing about the gas was that the moment it hit him, Traveler became totally and completely aware of the world around him for the first time in his life. That was the whole idea, of course. Eventually, the gas would make you so painfully conscious of every fibre of your body that you'd hear everything, feel everything, smell everything. Your own heartbeat would drive you crazy. The general idea behind the gas was to reduce entire armies into raving lunatics.

Traveler and his team were lucky. The guerrillas found them surrounded by corpses and crazies out there in the jungle and called in the real spooks. The Agency boys got them back to the States, and there Traveler got real lucky. His doctors came up with an experimental antidote that retarded the gas's degenerative effect.

He never did find out what happened to Hill, Orwell, and Margolin. He would find out though. He'd find them and save them.

Traveler doubled over as Aikers hit him one last time for good measure.

"Sit him down over there," Aikers instructed his Cro-Magnons. The captain waddled over to a large chair and eased himself into a cushioned seat.

"Now that we've been introduced . . . let's talk."

Traveler slumped in a straight-backed wooden chair, the towering, uniformed goons standing on either side of him. Something in the back of his head clicked. Somewhere nearby, a woman was suffering. He could sense it. He tasted blood. The pain in his stomach was overwhelming. Shut down. Compartmentalize. Isolate the hurt. Fight it, damn it. Fight it. Shove it down, deeper. Deeper. Hide it. Obliterate it.

He faced Aikers. The pain was receding. Fading. Fading. Fading.

He took a deep breath. He knew his chest was bruised, but now a veteran at this process, he no longer felt the ruptured flesh's pulsations.

The captain was thrown by the sight of the amazingly clear-eyed, conscious stranger before him. "What can I do for you?" Traveler inquired.

"Who are you?"

"No one."

"What do you want here?"

Traveler shrugged. He wanted nothing. Expected nothing. Demanded less.

Aikers was simmering. "You killed three of my men today."

"They were assholes."

"That's beside the point. You killed them."

Traveler said nothing further. The captain began floating around the small office. "The amazing thing is you did it all in a quick, clean kill. They were armed. You were not. I'm impressed."

35

Traveler stared out the window. The main street was empty. The woman's torment reverberated in the back of his mind.

The captain continued waddling, clasping his pudgy hands behind his back. "Don't bliss out. I have men who could do the same. You do it for money, right?"

"Or gold or gas or a box of .45 ACP if you got one."

"Who do you work for?"

"Myself . . . or whoever pays me."

Aikers smiled, his jowls bunching up as his lips expanded. "And Milland? Did he offer to pay you?"

Traveler saw no sense in denying the obvious. "He made me an offer."

"Did you accept?"

"I said I'd think about it."

Aikers nodded, suddenly resembling a bulldog. "Good move. Good move. It's always wise to keep your options open. Before the war I lived by that credo. I thrived on chance, on danger. I made daring choices. I was climbing the ladder of success, I was. Indeed, I was one of the most sought-after CPA's in Seattle. Yes, indeed. It was only a matter of time before some accounting firm with vision made me a full partner. Then, this blasted war happened. Well, I was already a local legend in the Guard, so I rushed to the aid of my country, didn't I? And I survived. Many didn't. But I got my men safely through it, didn't I? I hid them in places most civilians didn't know about. That proves I'm a born leader, doesn't it. Lead I have. Lead I will."

He waddled over to Traveler and grabbed him by the hair. "I may not look like much to you, merce, but I'm respected by my men. What I lack in muscle I make up in brainpower. Brainpower. That's the name of the survival game. Others have perished. I prosper."

Traveler found a window behind the man's elbow and stared out of it. The main street was still empty. Odd, that.

Aikers released his hold and turned toward the

window. "I know. You're regular army. You're not impressed by my weekend warriors. Well, you should be. My men are combat vets with fifteen years of fighting behind them. Fifteen years of battles and we've more than come through them in one piece. We've actually grown in ranks. I've recruited some excellent new guardsmen, haven't I."

He leaned against the window ledge, resting his palms on the dusty sill. "But I'm tired of moving around. Right now, this looks like a good spot to settle in. More than that, it seems a good spot to branch out from. Are you hearing what I'm telling you?"

"It sounds familiar . . . yes."

"We've put up with a lot of shit for fifteen years, now. It's time that we got what we deserve. And we deserve this town. All we want to do is live out our natural lives in peace. That's all."

"That's all?"

"Well, of course, to do that, we can't have outsiders interfering."

"Outsiders like me?"

"Outsiders like Milland!" The stocky, sweaty guardsman turned and faced Traveler meaningfully. "He represents everything that was bad in this country . . . candy-assed bureaucrats!"

Traveler nodded at the CPA-turned-warrior.

Aikers folded his arms across his chest. "I have plans. Great plans. Plans for expansion. Plans for rebuilding! I need able bodies to help me carry out those plans. Whatever Milland offered you, I'll double!"

"Not interested."

Aikers chuckled, making strange, pig-noises through his nose. "Refuse and I'll kill you."

Traveler sighed. Subtlety in bargaining did not seem a strong point of the locals. "Milland offered me whatever supplies I needed."

"If you agree to spy on Milland for me, I'll give you more supplies than you can use in two lifetimes!"

A look at Aikers's beaming face revealed that the commander obviously felt that he had just made Traveler an offer he couldn't refuse. A sudden pain tingled sharply above Traveler's right eye. The woman was experiencing great pain. Pain comparable to the horror Traveler had dealt with in El Hiagura. The mercenary wondered, briefly, if Margolin, Hill, and Orwell were still alive. And, if they were alive, how had they dealt with their wounds? Had their nervous systems exploded? Had they been reduced to madmen?

Aikers was looming before him. Traveler shrugged. For the time being, he'd do whatever was necessary to remain alive. "Agreed."

A grin spread across the chubby man's face like red ink on a blotter. Aikers had more gums in his mouth than teeth, which wasn't uncommon. It seemed like dentists were among the first to go. "Excellent!" the leader of men exclaimed. "Excellent."

Aikers motioned the two guardsmen goons away from Traveler. Traveler stood, slowly. The pain in his midsection from the beating had all but disappeared.

Aikers stared up at the man. "I just can't let you walk out of here, you know. Milland probably saw my men take you away. Indeed, he's probably wondering exactly what we've been talking about all this while. Now, what can I do about that? Let's see. While I *do* want you to work for me, I have to take into account that you killed three of my men in cold blood."

Aikers stood there for a moment. "I have it! A solution that should satisfy everyone!"

He quickly unsheathed a showy bayonet and slashed through the air, catching Traveler below his right elbow. Blood spurted from the wound. Traveler was too shocked by the move to actually experience pain. Aikers was ecstatic.

"That will show Milland how I feel about you! That will show you what I'm capable of! Everyone is happy. Hee. Hee. Hee. Hee."

Traveler stared at the giggling guardsman. The two goons pushed him out of the room and down the hallway. He passed a pale yellow door. A sudden wave of nausea told him that the woman in pain was being held captive inside. She was young. She had been raped today. She would be raped again.

The guardsmen pushed him past the door.

Traveler pressed his hand down against the wound. Blood trickled down his arm and onto the floor. He could still hear Aikers chuckling. Hee. Hee. Hee. Hee.

Something inside Traveler snapped . . . ever so quietly. He'd see them all dead. Once more, he'd arrange it so they paid Traveler up front for their own funerals.

The grimace on Traveler's face slowly twisted itself into a tight-lipped grin. Hee. Hee. Hee. Hee. His ass.

# 5

Bellows, the bartender, couldn't believe his eyes when Traveler walked through the door.

"Why, it's Lazarus returned from the dead!"

"I need a drink. Fast." Traveler sat at a table in a darkened corner of the room. The blood on his arm was dry now, well clotted. He flexed his limb slowly. Chunks of blood flecked onto the floor.

Bellows walked over and placed a shot on the tabletop. He noted Traveler's wound. "Cut yourself shaving?"

"Don't you ever get tired of yourself?"

"Lots," Bellows acknowledged, pulling up a chair next to the stranger. "But I'm the best company I got. We black folks have to stick together."

Traveler glared at the bartender. Bellows heaved a sigh. "Guess you don't like our little town too much."

Traveler grunted, swilling down the shot.

"Well," Bellows said sadly, "what are you going to do? The people here are stuck. The people here aren't in control of the guns. That's Milland's and Aikers's territory. So, we just try to make the best out of a bad situation."

Traveler glared at the huge fellow. His ice-blue eyes peeled into Bellows's forehead. The barkeep turned his face away. "Okay, so it sucks."

The man leaned toward Traveler, resting his double

chin on his clublike hand. "So. Are you entering the gunrunning sweepstakes?"

"What?"

"Are you going after the shipment the Glory Boys are bringing through?"

"That must be the worst kept secret in the world."

"You don't keep secrets in towns like this, Lazarus. That's something to remember. And secrets about guns? Forget it. Guns mean power. Guns mean life."

"Or death."

The two men allowed the conversation to drift off as a sob cut through the air. A white-haired, handsome man sat at a table in the center of the room. He was drunk. He seemed to belong in that chair at that table in that spot; a fixture in the near-deserted bar.

Dressed in a battered suit, the man exuded a sense of rumpled elegance. Traveler instinctively knew that the man had been something once . . . but never would be again. There was a goodness there. Once there may even have been a strength, but now there was an overwhelming aura of decay. The man choked back another sob and poured the latest in a series of drinks from a near-empty bottle in front of him.

"Who's that?" Traveler inquired.

"Jim Beckman," Bellows whispered. "He used to be the mayor of this town. I suppose, technically, he still is. He kept this place going for years before the flotsam and jetsam arrived. It's a real shame. A real shame. Milland's right-hand man, Moon? He turned Beckman in. Moon used to be the mayor's aide. Moon saw a chance to be more of a conquering hero type with Milland and just let Beckman drift. Damn shame."

Bellows focused his hound-dog eyes on the drunken man. "Poor bastard. Milland takes over his town, and Aikers takes over his daughter."

Traveler remembered the strong female presence in the Aikers compound. "Daughter?"

"Melissa. She's only a kid. Nineteen, now. Twenty

41

tops. Aikers took a fancy to her when he came into town. He moved into city hall and took Melissa with him. She's been up there for quite a while, now. She tried to escape once, but he told her straight, if she didn't cooperate, the old man would get it."

"Has he tried to kill himself yet?"

"Has he ever. For the first year or so he was in the emergency ward about once a week. Now, he doesn't bother. He's usually too juiced."

Traveler took note of the deep lines on the mayor's forehead. He tried to imagine what it would be like to keep an entire city sane the day after Armageddon, and the day after that, fighting off the physical horrors of death and disease and the mental anguish that rides with it. And then, after winning those fights, to lose it all to a group of armed geeks.

Beckman, realizing that he was being scrutinized, turned his red-flecked eyes in Traveler's direction. "The damnable thing about it all," he announced, as if reading Traveler's thoughts, "is that I really *tried*. I really tried to do the right thing. Not what would just benefit a few of us . . . I tried to do what was best for the entire *town*. The right thing. I always tried to do the right thing."

Traveler soon realized that the mayor was talking to no one in particular. He shuddered. He had the feeling that he had just strolled into one of the largest insane asylums in existence. Hell, but the whole world struck him as being one Olympian laughing academy. In the back of his mind, he supposed, he had always pictured the human race as being a lot stronger than it had turned out to be. He had been wrong. Well, there you go.

He raised his glass and toasted the mayor. "To the right thing."

"The right thing," the mayor repeated numbly. Beckman took one long swallow. Brown liquid ran down the side of his mouth.

"His manners aren't quite what they used to be," Bellows noted.

Traveler stifled an impulse to hit the barkeep. He rose from the table and walked silently toward the door. He paused in the doorway and stared outside. The main street was still deserted. The Meat Wagon was still parked where he had left it. The bodies of the guardsmen had been removed. Only a few crimson puddles drying on the surface of the street betrayed any hint of their former existence.

Traveler stepped outside and climbed into the wagon. He started the engine and pulled the van carefully down the street, stopping in front of the town's lone hotel. The marquee in front of the inn read, Welcome Survivors. Traveler grunted in appreciation of the invite and the sardonic humor.

He swung the car into the parking lot next door and came to a halt next to a few burnt-out autos, a jeep in running condition, and something that used to be a cat.

Traveler reached into the back of the tear-shaped van and pulled a duffel bag forward. He took a small photo of four young, smiling soldiers surrounded by an unfamiliar jungle out of the glove compartment and dropped it into the bag. He checked to make sure that his weapons were placed securely in the gun rack mounted in the area where a passenger's seat used to be. He picked up his shotgun and placed it in the duffel bag.

He adjusted the crossbow on his back and stepped from the car, slamming the door and setting the trip wires. Stepping gingerly over the cat cadaver, he walked toward the front entrance of the hotel.

A sticker on the front door announced: We Take VISA, American Express, Master Charge, Diner's Club and Wampum.

Traveler shook his head in wonderment and stepped inside the lobby. It was a weird room. Dark and spacious, empty but for two winos sleeping it off on a couch next to an artificial fireplace. Traveler reckoned it had been

43

a collegiate cathedral in its day. Now, it smelled like dust and cat piss. The carpet must have been green at one time. It sure wasn't now.

Plastic potted palms defied the lack of sun. Muzak drifted eerily through the air. A calendar from 1989 still hung on a wall near the door. The square designated December 20, 1989, was circled in red with the words "Big Blow-Out" scrawled over it. Framed portraits of the city's college in its formative years as well as several paintings of children with large bug-eyes were scattered on other walls.

The place was a tribute to antique Americana. All it needed was a couple of lawn jockeys and a pink flamingo to make it complete.

Traveler sighed and approached the front desk. Seated in a chair perched before a wall of empty mail slots was a woman. A redhead. She smiled at Traveler. She had a nice face. There was just too much of it. He figured she weighed in at about the same general area as his car.

The cherubic woman grinned at the stranger. "Let me guess. You want a room, right?"

Traveler nodded.

"Another knight in shining armor," the woman muttered.

"You get a lot of them in here?"

"We get them all in here, honey. Where else are they going to go? You boys come in all shapes, sizes, and mental denominations. We get the ex-military men, the former mafiosi, the assassins, the free-lance survivalists. Every piece of garbage imported to this town winds up staying at Bess's hotel. They usually check out feet first, too."

"I'll try to use the stairs."

The woman behind the desk chuckled. In spite of her attempt at worldly, cynical detachment, Traveler noticed that she was fairly young and, beneath all that flesh, was more alive than anyone he'd seen so far. But he had the feeling that even her natural

44

energy had been sapped by years of living on fear and loneliness.

"You have a high turnover, I take it," Traveler said.

"You got it, bud."

"Don't any of your guests survive?"

She shook her head from side to side. "No way."

Traveler cocked an eyebrow inquisitively.

Bess shrugged her titanic shoulders. "You didn't hear this from me, blue eyes. Both Aikers and Milland have pretty tight-knit groups. They don't trust any of the new recruits they hire . . . especially the good ones. Hey, who's to know how long you guys will stay bought? So, they use you and lose you."

Traveler smiled thinly. "So they hire you for a job. And if the enemy doesn't get you . . ."

". . . your employers will, sweetcakes."

Traveler motioned for a key. "How do I pay you?"

"Don't worry about it. Both Aikers and Milland pay my upkeep. It's to their advantage. They like to keep an eye on their shootists, and this hotel is right in the open."

She handed Traveler his key. "Who sent for you?"

"No one."

"Who are you working for?"

"Myself."

Bess flashed a toothy grin at Traveler. "Great. An entrepreneur, eh?"

Traveler took the key and headed for the elevator, carrying his duffel bag over his back.

"I shouldn't tell you this," Bess called after him, "but . . . those guardsmen you eradicated this afternoon?"

Traveler stopped mid-step, his back still to the front desk.

Bess finished her thought. "Two of their friends are waiting upstairs for you. In front of your room, most likely. I wouldn't give them a key."

Traveler turned to her, somewhat confused.

She laughed at his naïve expression. "It was no secret

45

you'd wind up here, Tonto. Like I said, all roads lead to Bess's. Just think of those two as your official welcome wagon."

Traveler nodded. "Thanks."

"Try not to shoot up the wall, huh? It's hard to get plasterers these days."

Traveler looked at the key in his hand: Room 309. An elevator opened in the lobby before him. He leaned inside, pressed the button marked 3, and quickly pulled himself out of the lift as the doors began to close. Traveler made a quick left and leaped up the carpeted stairway, double-timing it up to the third floor. En route, he pulled the combat knife from the sheath hanging from his belt. It was a knife he had grown used to using. A knife that silently, swiftly, would cut through almost anything . . . or anybody.

Traveler silently made his way to the top of the third floor landing. He peered around the corner of the stairway. Two wild-eyed men with crew cuts in badly wrinkled national guard uniforms waited eagerly next to the elevator. One had an elderly double-barrel 12-gauge, the other a gleaming Louisville slugger. Traveler got ready for another round of the Game.

He stared at the pair. Traveler had no respect for men who killed for fun or power. Especially when they did it so badly.

Traveler only killed to survive.

Like an animal.

The elevator opened. The two men readied themselves to pounce on its passenger. Finding none inside, they hesitated, gaping at the empty car.

They backed away from the lift, and the door closed. Confused, they stood in the middle of the hallway. Traveler eased his duffel bag down and trotted down the carpeted corridor, his knife poised in his left hand.

He didn't make a sound. One of the guardsmen whirled suddenly, and spotting Traveler, tried to bring the shotgun's gaping barrels to bear. Traveler slashed at the man's biceps. The man yelled in both surprise and pain as a fountain of crimson shot across the hallway and he spun away. The knife headed toward the guardsman a second time, skewering his kidney. Within ninety seconds, he'd be quite dead.

The other guardsman dropped the bat and attempted a ham-handed assault on Traveler with a four-and-one-quarter Dirk knife, a small but lethal weapon when found in the right hands. The square-jawed geek made a swing at Traveler's eyes. His aim was bad, and the blade passed harmlessly by. Traveler stepped backwards . . . allowing his assailant's momentum to draw him in. The guardsman stumbled forward. Traveler held out his combat knife. He felt the knife blade slide upward through the flesh of the man's neck.

The man collapsed, bloodily, in a heap at Traveler's feet.

Traveler sighed, wiped the blade of the knife on the corpse's trousers, and pushed the elevator button. The lift arrived, and when the doors arthritically opened, Traveler rolled the two men inside and pushed the button marked L.

He returned to his bag, picked it up, and proceeded to room 309. Unlocking the door, he cautiously entered the small, drab cubicle and checked it for any further well-wishers. Finding none, he called down to Bess at the front desk.

"You have two guardsmen on the way down," Traveler informed her.

"Are they checking out?" she asked.

"Afraid so."

"The usual way?"

"Uh-huh."

Bess paused for a moment. "How bad is my carpet?"

"Pretty bad. No gunplay, though."

"Well, thanks for that. The wallpaper pattern is a bitch to try to replace."

Traveler hung up the phone. A chill made a surprise

arrival throughout his frame. The room seemed to grow smaller around him. He yanked open the window. There was a two-foot-wide ledge outside, towering three stories above the town's main street.

Nice view.

Darkness was falling. Aikers wasn't going to like losing two more of his men. On the other hand, Milland would probably pay Traveler a bonus for two extra guardsmen eliminated.

Traveler stared at the Dirk, the bat, and the shotgun lying harmless on his bedspread.

He would probably turn a profit from the killings.

Does anyone play baseball anymore? he wondered.

# 6

Roberta Paxton scolds the tiny dachshund cowering in the corner of the kitchen.

"Bad Maddy. Bad dog." The dog, its woeful eyes trained on the attractive young blond woman, makes a few halfhearted whining noises. It's all Roberta can do not to laugh.

"Eating little Kiel's cookie when you have a bowl of your own food right in front of you!"

Roberta tries to put a scowl on her face but settles for a smirk. She walks across the linoleum-tiled kitchen carrying the half-eaten oreo in her hand. She drops the cookie in the trash bag. While her back is toward the dog, Maddy slinks out of the kitchen doorway and into the yard.

A little boy, his hair the color of freshly cut straw, toddles into the room. "Maddy bad. Maddy take cookie!" he declares solemnly.

Roberta smiles at her son. He's getting more like his father every day. Kiel has her hair but his father's ice-blue eyes. His father's stance. Soon, her husband would be home again. Out of the jungle, forever.

Roselle Park, New Jersey, wasn't such a bad town to start a family in, actually. A little seedy. Not too sophisticated. Solidly blue-collar. But it's close to New York, and if you didn't mind the presence of the nearby oil refineries along the highway . . .

49

Outside in the yard, the dachshund begins to howl. Roberta, puzzled, looks out the kitchen window. As she does so, a bright flash illuminates the sky. It's coming from the north. Newark? New York? It can't be an explosion from the refinery.

Roberta stares directly into the light. She feels her eyes burn, white-out, cease to function. She is blind. "Oh my god!" she screams. "Oh my god!" She backs up across the room, tripping over little Kiel. The child begins to cry. The dog continues to howl.

A fierce gust of white-hot wind tears through the house. Roberta's flesh begins to bubble. Kiel emits one, long screech. The dog stops howling as the house blows apart.

The same blast of heat that disintegrates the house ignites the nearby oil refinery. Acres of tanks erupt into a titanic fireball. The volcanic wind now abruptly changes direction, whipping backwards 180 degrees, pulling the debris it had tossed southward back north.

What was once a densely populated area is now desolate. Swirling fire storms explode everywhere. They feed on the heat. On the wind. On the bodies. Cries and screams echo, feebly, everywhere. Neighbors stumble over the remains of neighbors. Minds go numb as the survivors are forced to take in the enormity of what they are experiencing. Faces are twisted and charred. Bodies are covered with oozing flash burns.

A vital, laughing being once called Roberta is now nothing more than a smoldering heap of flesh. The shadow-shape composed of ashes and bone chips sprawled alongside was once a child with hair the color of straw.

In the distance a massive mushroom cloud continues a seemingly endless ascent skyward, dwarfing all the fires, all the destruction around it. New York City is gone. Most of northern New Jersey is an inferno. Slices of Connecticut and Pennsylvania are simply erased from the face of the earth. The cloud continues to spiral upward. The air moans one last time.

"Breakfast."

The cloud picks up hunks of debris, pulverizing them instantly.

"Breakfast."

Bess stood in the open doorway of room 309. The room was empty. The bed was not slept in. The window was open. The portly woman heard a moan from outside. She ran to the window. Outside, Traveler lay asleep on the ledge, a blanket pulled up to his chin. He was shaking. Sweating. Low, anguished mumbles escaped his lips.

Instinctively, Bess reached out and touched the man. The feeling of flesh on his sensitive skin sent an ice pick plunging through his heart. He awoke with a start. Sitting straight up on the narrow ledge, he suddenly remembered who he was, where he was, and when he was. He relaxed, slightly.

He turned and faced the red-haired cherub. "Do you always barge into people's rooms unannounced?"

"I announced," Bess replied. "I guess I wasn't loud enough to be heard by my resident human fly."

The woman retreated and walked toward the door, expressing no surprise at Traveler's unorthodox sleeping habits. Traveler climbed back inside, dragging his blanket in with him. "I don't like being confined," he said by way of explanation.

"I figured as much," Bess said, pausing in the doorway. "Don't worry, mister. It doesn't faze me. I've seen all kinds of heebie-jeebies in here. Delayed stress. Shell shock. Battle fatigue. Drug addiction. DTs. You name it, I've seen it. Funny though. You're only the second guy to try sleeping on a ledge."

Traveler blinked. "Second? Who was the first?"

"Just another drifter. He was a lot like you. You don't like being touched. I can tell. This guy didn't either. It wasn't that he was antisocial. It was as if being touched *hurt* him, caused him a lot of actual pain."

"How long ago was he here?"

"A year. Year and a half maybe."

"Would you recognize him again?"

"Would I ever. Big guy. Black. Crazy eyes. Scar halfway down his face. Not your basic pretty-boy type."

Traveler rummaged through his duffel bag, pulling out the photo of the four smiling soldiers. He handed it to Bess. "Yeah," she said, nodding. "That's my boy. Hey. Is this you? Must have been taken before the war, huh? You were pretty handsome then, mister."

She handed him back the photo. "You look like hell, now."

Traveler returned the picture into his duffel bag. Orwell was alive. And if Orwell was still kicking around, maybe Hill and Margolin were, too.

"You looking for the guy?" Bess asked.

"When I can."

"Yeah. You two are from the same mold, all right. Real independent types. Milland and Aikers both wanted him to work on their teams. He told them both to take a hike. He took about a dozen of their men out while saying good-bye."

"He got out of town alive?"

"Oh, yeah. He was alive, all right. Not real happy but very alive."

Traveler cocked his head inquisitively. "Not happy?"

"Yeah. He always seemed to be in a lot of pain. He didn't hide his as well as you do yours. He was always twitching. Jumpy as a cat on a hot plate. Didn't sleep much. You had the feeling that he *couldn't* sleep but that he'd love to. He was pretty fucked up. I figure that you're crazy but you're not that scrambled."

Traveler almost smiled. "You mentioned breakfast?"

"Yeah. Got some powdered eggs downstairs. It's a real treat, believe me. The restaurant down the block serves up dog food."

"I know."

"Well, shake your ass downstairs before the eggs blow away. And do me a favor, will you? Try not to toss in your sleep. I got a tough enough time keeping the inside of this mausoleum clean without having to worry about scraping you off the outside."

Bess walked briskly out of the room. Traveler sat down on the bed with a sigh. He was almost elated. Maybe, just maybe, he had a sense of purpose in his life again.

Fifteen years ago, following the neurotoxin incident, he and his buddies had been sent to separate stateside hospitals for debriefing and treatment. The President's enemies in Congress figured that they had caught Frayling meddling in international affairs in a manner that could lead to impeachment. Traveler and his friends would be held up as living examples of what a devious weasel the President was. Unfortunately, the nuke-out put an end to the impeachment proceedings, the war in El Hiagura, and political life in general.

When Traveler fled from the hospital, he took all the vials of his experimental antidote he could find with him. Stealing a small refrigerator, he installed it back in the Meat Wagon. In the back of his mind, he always entertained the notion that one day he'd find Orwell, Hill, and Margolin and be able to administer the medicine before the degenerative process forced them into total insanity.

For fifteen years that idea had been nothing more than a pipe dream. But, now, with Bess's story still ringing in his ears, that dream was rapidly moving toward reality.

Traveler dressed quickly. He strapped his crossbow to his back and his knife around his waist. For the first time in ages, he felt like whistling.

His good mood was short-lived, however. He swung open the door to leave and found himself face-to-face with three fairly ugly individuals. A tall, buzzard-like guy was holding a shotgun. Everybody loved shotguns nowadays. If you could mix up a little black powder and shove it and some metal bits into an old shell, you had a gun again. The barrel was aimed at Traveler's midsection.

"I didn't ring for room service." Traveler smiled, gently pointing the gun barrel away from him with the forefinger of his left hand.

"Mr. Milland wants to see you," a ferret type stated.

"I'll be over after breakfast."

The tiny ferret would not be swayed by logic. "He wants to see you now!"

Traveler sighed. Before the man with the shotgun could react, he reached over and snatched the diminutive man by the throat, lifted him high, and placed him directly in front of the buzzard's gun. The man with the shotgun immediately realized that if he fired at Traveler, the chances were good to excellent that he'd blow his short friend into several shorter pieces. The buzzard-man gulped. His Adam's apple seemed to do a somersault.

The ferret, still suspended above the floor, glared angrily at Traveler. "Well. Okay. But you'd better eat fast."

Traveler lowered the little man to the ground. Milland's trio loped off down the hallway.

Traveler took the stairway down to the lobby. There was a near-deserted coffeehouse next to the front desk. In it, Bess sat at the only table boasting a tablecloth. She spooned what looked like watery tapioca into her lipstick-encased mouth. The substance on her fork, allegedly eggs, slipped down between the utensil's prongs.

"I started without you," she said as Traveler walked over.

Traveler sat down across from her. His plate was filled with the slimy yellow substance. He prodded it tentatively with his fork.

"Oh, by the way," Bess said casually. "One of Aikers's boys brought you a present."

She raised a small cardboard box from the seat next to her and placed it on the tabletop.

Traveler stared at it. "What do you think it is?"

Bess took a sip of what passed for coffee. "A bomb, most likely."

Traveler snatched the box, stared at it for a long second, and tossed it through an open window, bracing himself.

Nothing happened.

He stared at the portly woman, still struggling with her eggs. "You could have been wrong."

Bess smiled sweetly. "Don't think so."

A sudden blast rocked the coffeehouse. The explosion wasn't powerful enough to shatter the windows. It just rattled the panes.

"Aikers's boys have always been rotten at homemade explosives," she commented, getting up from the table. Traveler stared, slack-jawed, at the rotund hotel owner. It struck him that he might have stumbled onto the first postholocaust guru.

Traveler pushed his eggs aside and headed out toward the lobby. Bess stood behind the coffee shop's counter, a smile on her face. "You may not be real popular in this town," she said, "but you sure make life interesting."

# 7

Brown morning sunlight filtered into the window behind Milland's desk. Traveler sat glumly in front of the
tall, distinguished man.

"I don't approve of your methods," said Milland,
looking like he'd just tasted some of Bess's so-called
eggs. "I don't approve of them at all. You've turned this
town into a three-ring circus in less than a day."

Traveler did not reply. He was depressed by the
sense of finality in the room.

Milland began to drone on about his hatred of Aikers,
and while he approved of Traveler's treatment of the
guardsmen, he would appreciate it if he, Traveler, would
just cool out a bit. Milland blathered on, but Traveler
heard no more than the buzz of his voice.

It wasn't the presence of death, per se, that Traveler
felt, but rather the aura of great and total stagnation.
Milland was a man who cared nothing about forward
motion. He cared nothing about the world outside. He
cared nothing about the future. All he valued was control.
And, in a world scarred by radioactive debris, destruction,
and horror, Traveler couldn't see that control meant a
hell of a lot.

The only thing of value in the postholocaust world
was human life.

Yet, Milland didn't realize it.

Men like Milland seldom did.

As much as he hated to admit it, Traveler did value life. Still. In spite of everything he had been through. Despite the lives he had taken. Maybe *because* of everything he had been through and the lives he had taken, he valued life above all things. At times, he entertained the notion that the war had actually happened for a reason. Maybe humanity had to bomb itself back into the near Stone Age to see what a piece of work it was.

Sometimes it took the spectre of death to make people notice just how wondrous life could be. Traveler remembered being in the jungle, hiding behind the bushes, watching a group of kids tossing hand grenades into a lake. *Whooomp. Whooomp. Whooomp.* It was one of the scariest, funniest things he had ever seen. Hill had sat next to him.

"Why don't we kill them?"

"What for?"

"They're the enemy, man. They're armed."

Traveler had just cracked up, laughing. "Man, haven't you done jungle work before? Those kids aren't the enemy. They're just kids."

"Then what are they doing with those grenades?"

"Man, they're just fishing. They're just fishing."

Traveler had watched the kids dive into the lake and retrieve their catch. He was glad he was on point that day. Maybe another soldier would have cut them down, panicking at the sound of grenades. To Traveler that sight was just as beautiful as watching his own kid sitting near a fishing hole with a pole. Life was life. Precious.

Four hours later he had found the kids' bodies on the roadside. Guerrilla got them, most likely. Traveler hadn't saved their lives. Only postponed their execution.

Traveler blinked as the buzzard and ferret came into the room.

Hell. Maybe the last war was just a historical joke. Maybe the whole world was destined to go down the toilet so assholes like these could roam free.

"Yes, bring him up here immediately," Milland said to his overeager henchmen. The two scurried out of the room, casting venomous glances at Traveler. As the two men exited, a tall, bald-headed man strolled regally in.

"Ah, Moon. I believe you've met our newcomer." Milland smiled. "Thomas Moon, this is our newest recruit. He calls himself Traveler, I believe."

Moon extended a hand. "Hello again."

Fighting the temptation to make a misanthropic gesture, Traveler gingerly shook the man's hand. Shards of pain shot through his arm as he did so.

Traveler gazed into the man's eyes, realizing that this was the trusted aide who had betrayed the mayor and the town.

Milland motioned for Moon to sit next to Traveler.

"We have reason to believe that the arms shipment we've been waiting for will pass this way as early as tonight."

"Indeed," Moon said without betraying any hint of strong interest.

"Where did you pick up that information?" Traveler asked.

"A paid informant, of course." Milland smiled.

"Of course," Traveler repeated.

"Moon, I'd like you and Traveler to go out with Palm and Idle tonight and scout around. See if you can spot the Glory Boys. Without them spotting you, if you can. Reconnoiter their position and report to me. We'll move out with the men necessary to wipe them out as quickly as we can. We must beat Aikers and whatever road scum are in the area to these guns."

"Yes, sir," Moon said, gazing at a point on the wall somewhere behind and above Milland's head. Jesus, Traveler thought, the guy is actually bored!

Traveler wasn't pleased with Milland's plan at all. "I was hired to scout. I do that alone," he said.

"You were hired to work for me. Period. How I use you is my business," Milland informed him.

Traveler glanced at Moon. The bald fellow managed an almost-smirk. Apparently, he was used to Milland's dictatorial ways. Traveler decided to drop the argument. He was playing in someone else's ball field.

The door to Milland's office burst open. The ferret and the buzzard walked in, dragging an emaciated piece of human debris between them. The roadrat was young. He couldn't have been more than fourteen years old. He had a withered arm and an alabaster, vacant eye. The kid was a mutant. The first generation to be born after the war didn't fare too well. Some were put to death shortly after birth. Others, like this kid, weren't so fortunate.

Traveler took in the scene. At one point in time he would have felt instant sympathy for the gangly kid. But he'd roamed across too much of postnuke America for too long and seen too much of the kind of revenge this generation of monsters took on the country to feel anything like that now.

He detached himself emotionally from the room and made mental notes. He realized that the boy being tossed in front of Milland may be young, but he was experienced. He wasn't to be trusted, no matter how large the bribe he was being offered. Roadrats were vicious, unpredictable, and immoral. They were, however, fanatically loyal to their tribe. A roadrat, a true roadrat, would never betray his mob.

Traveler was about to mention this fact to Milland when he thought better of it. Milland wouldn't pay any attention to anything the world-weary mercenary said. He was too caught up in his monomaniacal quest for power.

The ferret and the buzzard stood at the boy's back.

Milland looked into the kid's one good eye. "You've actually seen the Glory Boys?"

"Seen 'em yesterday. Told you that," the boy said from between blistered lips.

Milland addressed Moon. "We caught him yesterday

wandering a little too close to our barbed wire. Didn't we, boy?"

"You did." The roadrat nodded. "You did."

Traveler realized that the boy would say anything to get out of Milland's grasp. The kid probably knew about as much about the Glory Boys and their rifles as Traveler did: which meant that he knew nothing more than what Milland had babbled.

"You have nothing more to add?" Milland asked.

"No," the roadrat said. "They're comin' from up north. They're maybe twenny miles from here. Told you that already. Pay me and let me go."

Traveler didn't like it. What was the kid doing here? He seemed too experienced to just walk into a setup like this. Something smelled funny about all this.

The ferret let out a yell. Traveler caught something going on between the roadrat and the ferret. The rifle was the center of the struggle. Traveler couldn't tell if the boy was grabbing it or pushing it away. Suddenly, Moon produced a forty-five. He fired one shot. The explosion sent the top half of the boy's face flying across the room and against the wall. It hit with a smack and slowly oozed its way down to the floor. The roadrat's body toppled onto the floor in front of Milland's desk, pumping blood furiously.

Milland stood there, tall, gaunt, and although outwardly impassive, obviously annoyed.

"Christ, Moon," he said evenly. "I told you. Never in my office. Never in my office."

Moon nodded toward the ferret. "If Palm hadn't lost his gun."

"He grabbed it from me. Everybody seen it. Everybody."

Milland stared at the twitching body in front of him. "Get that out of here and bring in a mop."

The ferret and the buzzard removed the mess. Milland looked at Moon and Traveler. "You know what you're supposed to do."

Moon nodded.

"Then get out of here."

Moon and Traveler stood and left the room. Walking down the hall, they passed the ferret and the buzzard scurrying along with a mop and pail.

"Are those the guys we're scouting with tonight?" Traveler asked.

Moon nodded. "Idle and Palm. What do you think?"

Traveler said nothing. Trouble. Big trouble.

# 8

"Ever think about power?" Moon asked. Traveler watched the setting sun. He leaned up against the Meat Wagon. He shook his head from side to side.

"No," Moon said thoughtfully. "You don't strike me as the type who would. Power is a wonderful thing, though. Get enough power and you can grab onto experiences so wild that you've never even imagined them. Yeah. Power is something else. It's strange, though, how power affects different people. Some can handle it. Some can't."

Traveler watched the ferret and the buzzard walk over to the car. "And some wouldn't know it if it bit them in the ass," Traveler concluded.

Palm and Idle were in the midst of a whiney argument as they entered the parking lot next to the hotel.

"Why can't we all go in your car?" the buzzard named Idle bleated at Traveler.

Traveler turned his back on the man and opened the driver's door of the Meat Wagon. "The car's too small. I can take one extra. No more."

As he stooped to get into the car, Traveler caught a glimpse of movement at the far side of the parking lot. One of Aikers's guardsmen was watching him. He caught the man's eye and nodded in a conspiratorial manner. Let the geek report back to Aikers that Traveler was doing as he was told—spying on Milland.

62

"Come on," Traveler said to Moon.

Traveler climbed into the driver's seat, cleared the ammunition bag and the weapons out of the passenger's side, and opened the other door to the wagon. Moon lowered himself inside.

"You'll have to sit on the floor," Traveler said.

Moon sat in lotus position as Palm and Idle continued their whining outside. Traveler rolled down the window. "We take two vehicles, or you two stay behind. And if you *do* stay behind, have a great time explaining to Milland why you're not out with us tracking down Glory Boys."

The two men shut up and walked sullenly over to a '63 Chevy Impala. It was white with a blue fender and a right rear door so bashed in it was unopenable. The car burned gas like crazy and was made during a period when American cars were still as heavy as most small tanks. The Impala was probably real good at smashing through things and emerging more or less intact but pathetic as a pursuit vehicle.

Traveler revved up the wagon and headed out of town. Two guards, one of Aikers's men and one of Milland's, removed a wooden barricade at the end of the street, allowing both the wagon and the Impala to venture out into what passed for the real world.

The extent of the visual jolt was surprising to Traveler, who, although being caught within the boundaries of the town for only one day, had grown used to its outward normalcy. Paved streets. Rows of shops. Houses.

Now, here he was faced with postnuclear reality once again.

He didn't like it.

The wagon sped along the macadam highway. The air was a curtain of dust and grit. The sun shone, tarnished, through the layers of sand. Dead cars, a few with skeletal drivers, lined the roadside in various stages of decay.

Traveler tried to keep his eyes on the road ahead. It was a schizophrenic panorama that loomed before him. High above the swirling sand was a blue sky, peppered with careening cumulus clouds. The clear sky high above stirred up memories of tranquility, of Sunday afternoons in crowded parks in the days before hot spots and roadrats.

Traveler shook the memories clear of his head. Dangerous thoughts, those. First you'd be thinking of the clouds. Then, the picnics. Then, the wife. Then, the kid. Before long you wouldn't know if you wanted to cry or scream or lash out at something or someone with your bare hands or worse. He'd done all those things in the first years. Done them enough times to know better. Then done them till he burned out.

Moon, still seated cross-legged on the floor, seemed to sense Traveler's anger. He pointed to a blue-screened device on the dashboard. "That a radiation detector?"

"Yeah," Traveler acknowledged.

"Install it yourself?"

"Uh-huh."

Moon glanced in the back of the car. "Nice job you've done on this. It's a regular fortress."

"I like it."

"These bulletproof vests lining the back walls. They keep out more than the rain?"

"Uh-huh."

Moon scanned the interior. "Iron shutters across the windows. False bottom in the back. For ammo?"

"And tires when I can find them."

"Four-wheel drive?"

"Yeah, and a little Wankel engine that can run on anything from gasoline to good Scotch—anything with enough alcohol or oil in it."

"Good mileage?"

"Thirty-five miles to the gallon if the fuel is good. Twenty if it's not."

"How many gallons does it hold?"

"I've got a fifty-gallon tank."

"That gets you halfway across the country. What do you do then?"

"I've got a fuel bladder in the back for an extra fifty gallons, too."

"Nice. What would someone have to give you to get you to let go of this thing?"

Traveler thought a moment. "His life."

Moon lapsed into silence.

Traveler stared at the compass on his dashboard. The roadrat said that the Glory Boys were arriving from due north. That made no sense, though. Bellows, the barkeep, had said that Salt Lake City had been completely nuked out. That would mean that the northern area of the state would be one big hot spot. Okay. If the roadrat was lying . . . why was he lying? Did he just want to get out, get paid, or was he doing something more?

Moon remained silent. The Meat Wagon approached the remains of a shopping mall. Most of the outer walls had collapsed. All that was left of the sprawling structure were the exposed facades of the stores and arcades, a vast tiled expanse of sandblasted concrete benches and a dried-out fountain.

Traveler glanced in the mirror. The Impala was keeping pace. He checked the compass on his dash. He continued heading north, against his better judgment.

An explosion rocked the wagon.

"Shit," Traveler muttered. "Roadrats."

Oh well, at least he knew why the kid had lied. The air around him was shattered by the sound of primitive battle cries and rapid gunfire. Bullets sizzled by the car, pinging into the road.

Moon got to his knees and peered out the side window. "Christ! There must be a hundred of them!"

"Yeah," Traveler acknowledged. "There's a convention in the area. I suppose they want our cars. Can you handle a one-eighty?"

"Just give me one."

"In the back. Find it. Load it. Use it."

Moon leaned back to grab the rifle. A second explosion almost catapulted Moon through the wagon's roof.

Traveler swerved off the road and into the dirt, popping the wagon into four-wheel. "Don't worry. They won't harm the car if they can help it. They would like us out of the car and into the open, though."

A third blast rocked the car.

"RPG's," Traveler noted. "These guys are pretty well armed for rats.

"Hang on." Traveler hit the gas and sent the wagon fishtailing away from the road, farther into the dirt. He turned around, briefly. The Impala skidded and followed Traveler's lead. Bad move. The Chevy would have been better off hanging a quick U-turn, staying on the highway, and heading back to town with the cruise control set on *faster*. There was no way that lumbering car would hack it on the vast dirt vistas looming before it.

The roadrats poured out of the mall on foot, on motorcycles, bicycles, and on horseback. They brandished rifles, spears, and crudely fashioned longbows.

Traveler headed south, hoping to gradually swing back toward the city without the roadrats really noticing. The Impala was rapidly losing ground behind the wagon, hampered by both its weight and lack of maneuverability.

The roadrats fanned out behind the two vehicles, forming an inverted V shape. Traveler guessed that the rats would try to outflank the vehicles and then close ranks.

Bullets and arrows whizzed by the Meat Wagon. More than a few slapped into the van's sides. Maybe the rats were losing interest in the car. Moon cranked his window down an inch and stuck the rifle barrel outside. The Armalite AR-180 was a pretty effective light assault rifle, capable of smacking a target accurately at a distance of up to 450 yards. Its effectiveness was most lethal, however, within 150. None of the roadrats were that close . . . yet.

"Don't return their fire," Traveler warned. "Save it for later."

The Meat Wagon continued to speed forward.

The Impala plowed onward, bouncing wildly each time it hit a patch of uneven ground.

Before long, the large, lumbering auto was being paced on either side by a half dozen chopper-riding roadrats. The roadrats were dressed in rags and wearing long, flowing bandannas. It looked like a parody of a scene from an old John Ford western.

Traveler could see the panicked expression of the ferret behind the wheel. The buzzard fired wildly at the roadrats with a handgun. Too bad the fools forgot their shotgun. A pistol wasn't worth shit in that sort of encounter, and the way the man was firing, he'd be out of ammunition soon. Sure enough, Traveler saw the buzzard withdraw his hand from the window and bend over the gun to reload it.

At that point a bullet shattered the Impala windshield and the buzzard's head went jerking backwards and forwards twice. He slumped over the dashboard, the top of his head a mass of ruptured skin and exposed ooze.

The ferret had time to look over at his friend before the pane of glass on his left exploded under the impact of a projectile. The concussion sent the ferret tumbling onto the body of his dead compadre. The Impala fishtailed wildly for a moment before straightening. Because there was nothing in its way to slow it down, the Chevy continued to move onward.

The roadrats backed off from the vehicle, giving it plenty of room to decelerate. Realizing that the rats would be temporarily distracted, Traveler slammed his right foot down on the accelerator.

"Get ready," he told Moon. "We'll give them something to remember us by."

He swung the Meat Wagon around in a quick U, sending a plume of dust spiraling up toward an emerging night sky. The Meat Wagon charged at the line of choppers.

The roadrats, not expecting the quick role reversal, hesitated for a fatal moment. Rather than plow into the advancing line of rats headfirst, Traveler yanked the wheel, sending the Meat Wagon on a path which cut, horizontally, directly in front of the speeding bikers.

"Open fire," Traveler hissed as his car sliced in front of the rats' parade route. Moon did as he was told, spraying the advancing line with hot lead.

Traveler didn't bother to look to his right to see the effectiveness of his maneuver. He could hear the surprised yells and screams of the roadrats as their line of bikes collapsed.

He hit the gas and yanked the wheel, sending a spray of dirt and rocks onto the bodies of the fallen bikers.

Leaving them in his wake, Traveler glanced backwards briefly. Four dozen of the marauders were either out flat or staggering, wounded, next to their bikes. The roadrats still on horseback and bicycles attempted to close the pincers on the retreating Meat Wagon. Unfortunately, their fallen comrades were sprawled between their charge and Traveler. The attacking roadrats, finding their biker buddies either underfoot or blocking their way, wound up turning helplessly away.

Traveler continued to accelerate until the roadrats were far behind and the town was in view before him.

For once he didn't mind the thought of pulling into a highly populated area. He'd rather have a bad case of the heebie-jeebies than a terminal attack of roadrats.

Moon pulled the rifle barrel back into the car. "Some setup," he grunted.

Traveler said nothing. He was tired of setups. His whole life seemed to be a series of ambushes. Even now, as he speeded toward the supposed safety of the town, he knew he was leaving one setup for another.

The teenaged roadrat had led them right into a trap. Now, if a stranger in the area like Traveler had figured that out en route, why hadn't an experienced local fighting man like Moon? And if Moon had suspected foul play, why hadn't he mentioned it to Milland?

Traveler glanced at the man on his right. Even around other people, he felt totally alone.

# 9

Traveler sat in the hotel dining room, staring glumly at a mess of alleged stew on his plate. He was the only diner, aside from Bess. She showed no hesitation whatsoever at the prospect of digging into her generic dinner.

"I won't ask you why you're so late or what you've been up to," she said matter-of-factly. "If you want to get yourself killed, it's fine by me."

Traveler speared a hunk of what he assumed was meat. It dissolved as his fork touched it.

"What's eating you tonight?" she said, shoveling a forkful of the stuff into her ample mouth.

He moved his fork around the objects on his plate, half-expecting them to get up and walk away, insulted. "This town," he said. "Where the hell are all your people?"

"You want the whole, long story or the *Reader's Digest* version?"

Traveler shrugged. "I'm not going anywhere." He ran a shaking hand through his close-cropped hair.

Bess noted his agitation. "Having an attack of the fidgets again?"

Sweat was beginning to trickle down Traveler's brow. Very often he couldn't control these seizures. At times his nervous system just clicked in and clicked out. Right now he was beginning to overload. The events of the day were catching up to him. When he was alone, he could simply shut down, compartmentalize, go into an almost autistic, childlike trance. But around people, even friendly people like Bess, he couldn't let his guard down. After all, what was a warrior with a weakness?

A dead warrior, that's what.

Bess waddled out to the kitchen. "Hold tight, honey."

Traveler grasped the tabletop with his hands. Bess emerged with a bottle of tequila. She poured out a juice-glassful. "Here. Drink it down."

Traveler nodded meekly and downed the glass. It wasn't exactly the most scientific solution, but it worked. Whenever he grew overly hyper, a good depressant could sometimes bring him back down to mere manic level.

"Thanks," he muttered.

"Not at all," Bess said, once again digging into the mystery meal. "Well, where shall I begin?" she pondered. "Following the war, we all pretty much expected the worst, you know? The blowout occurred during college recess, so the town was half-empty. Only the townies and a few hundred students were left. Half of the faculty had already left for home as well.

"For some odd reason we weren't hit really hard. We're not really close to any major military installation, and sure as hell we're miles away from the major cities. The wind patterns were in our favor, too. They mostly blew the crap in the air northeast. So, we all just stayed indoors or in basements for a few months until the fallout was tolerable.

"With some of the faculty and most of the handymen still in town, we managed to keep the place running pretty smoothly. We all pitched in. Before the war I never ran a hotel. I was a high school English teacher up north. I was just here for a visit. Yeah, I used to bring knowledge to eager little minds."

Traveler grunted.

"Praise from a functional illiterate. Thanks. Well, the town was doing all right for a while. Then we started

71

noticing what was going on out there in the real world, you know? The scavengers, the roadrats, were getting pretty bold. They were organizing raids. They were after supplies and worse. Quite a few of the co-eds disappeared in the middle of the night. We'd find what was left of them scattered out by the old shopping mall.

"A bunch of the college boys and the local guys got a militia together. We ringed the town with whatever we could get our hands on and gathered whatever guns we had.

"We had the upper hand for a while. Mainly because we were fighting pretty addlebrained invaders. Hungry. Flash-burned. Desperate. Not military strategists. We picked up a lot of weapons from the dead. We were holding our own until . . ."

"The professionals showed up."

"You said it, honey. They descended on this burg like a plague of locusts. Within a month we had both Aikers and Milland encamped here. Of course, Milland was eased in thanks to our delightful Mr. Moon. Aikers just barged in. So, now, here we sit, with two kings at opposite ends of the block. Pretty quaint, eh?"

"And the people of the town did . . . nothing?"

Bess heaved a colossal sigh. "They did all they could, babe. Half of our fair-haired college boys were captured by Aikers's crew . . . or was it Milland's? It doesn't matter. They were led out into the college green and shot. Executed. That was intended to put a damper on our independent spirit. The rest of the militia, the men, are locked up in what used to be the college dining room. It's a regular hellhole now, straight out of the Spanish Inquisition. Half of those guys haven't been out in the fresh air, such that it is, in years. God knows what they're being fed. Each other, probably.

"There are a few of the older residents still living in their own homes. A couple of us townies are allowed to run businesses that are laughingly known as essential. What's left of the women are kept in the old college dorm. Our warriors screw them when they feel like it. At first some of the girls resisted. The college kids. The ones who resisted found themselves with their boyfriends out on the green collecting bullets and flies."

Traveler experienced a wave of nausea. He wondered if man had ever been a civilized creature to begin with. "What about children?"

"Ah, the children," Bess said, sadly. "We didn't have too many of them to begin with. About half of them were abused to death, literally. I suppose the survivors are growing up in our prison. And, of course, there have been by-products of our conquering heroes' escapades. Most of them . . ."

She took the fork from her mouth and put it on her plate. "Do you know that I used to cry all the time?"

Traveler stared into her eyes. They were sad but hard. "I can't anymore. I'm all tapped out," the woman continued. "The tears just won't come. And I don't know which is worse, the numbness or the tears. You see these kids being born. I mean, I still think it's possible for normal children to be brought into this world. I really do. But we haven't seen any of them being born here. Not yet, anyway. Most of the babies here haven't lived more than seventy-two hours. They were the lucky ones. A few lingered, but they were in pretty bad shape. They would never have made it for long."

"Mutants?"

"Poor sweet things."

"Were they killed?"

Bess nodded. "When we had a doctor, it was done painlessly. The man believed in euthanasia, and he did a very professional job. Quick. Painless. Or so I was told. Then, one of the gun-toting daddies objected to the doctor's interference and . . ."

"And . . ."

Bess picked up her fork. "And now we have no doctor."

"And the children?"

"None of them survive, but now they have time enough to hurt."

Traveler, his nerves steadying, got up and walked to the dining room counter, where the bottle of tequila sat. He poured a second glass. "A town with two would-be kings, two armies of goons, a populace under lock and key, and no one trying to do anything to change the situation. Jesus Christ! I thought El Hiagura was fucked up."

"It was." Bess smiled. "I read all about it in the newspapers, sweetcakes. And, please, don't play holier-than-thou with me. This town is screwed up. Granted. But, from what I gathered, so is ninety-nine percent of this burnt-out world. What can we do? We're stuck, my friend. There are still a lot of good people here. But they're not trained soldiers. They can't compete with the trigger-happy idiots who've nested in our midst."

She eyed Traveler meaningfully. "You know what the folks here need? They need a hero. They need a knight in shining armor to show them the way. We need a jouster of windmills, a slayer of dragons, a champion of the oppressed. And what do we get? We get *you*."

Traveler smirked and shook his head, placing his glass down on the counter. "I'm no knight in shining armor, lady. I'm no hero, either."

"No shit, Sherlock." Bess laughed, stirring her fork around her empty plate. "You look like hell, and you smell like worse. You're paranoid. Your nerves are shot. You got a chip on your shoulder the size of an oak, and you're a walking advertisement for gun control."

Bess flashed a beatific grin as Traveler returned to his seat. "But, times are tough. I guess you'll do."

# 10

Traveler didn't like the responsibilities connected with playing hero. A hero defended concepts that were right and honorable. That was beyond Traveler. Once upon a time, he had thought he knew what was right, what was worth fighting for. But that was a lifetime ago, a lifetime filled with names and sunrises and shiny cars and barking dogs with tails that wagged. A time when streets had shadows that weren't the outlines of bodies pulverized by an atomic mistake.

Traveler sat at the dining room table, deep in thought, when a short, squat shape materialized out of the shadows at the far end of the room.

Bess, busying herself at the counter, peered into the blackness. "Well, if my eyes do not deceive me, it's one of the pretenders to the local throne. Captain CPA."

Zeke Aikers marched into the room, his oily face glistening even brighter owing to a new layer of sweat. Traveler, still daydreaming, momentarily thought he was watching a newsreel of Mussolini strutting through the streets of Rome. Traveler blinked. Il Duce vanished. Aikers appeared.

Traveler eyed the man. He wondered how the little guy kept that one strand of hair wrapped around that chrome dome of his.

"I want to talk to you, Traveler," Aikers announced, pulling up a chair to the mercenary's right.

"So, talk," Bess called in a mock Yiddish accent. "Eat. Have a little something to drink. Wine? Tea? Cat piss?"

Aikers turned to the portly woman. "Can it, Bess. I can have you killed . . . or . . ."

Bess smiled sweetly. "Your men don't like raping fat women, Zeke. They wind up bouncing too much. It shakes 'em up too much. And they don't want to kill me because they like making their own beds even less."

The woman began whistling at the snack counter, languidly wiping the surface with a wet rag.

Aikers returned his attention to Traveler. "You went out with Milland's men today."

Traveler nodded. "Went out with three. Came back with one."

"You were supposed to keep me posted about Milland's moves."

"I didn't think it would be too smart for me to come running your way in broad daylight."

Aikers glared at the laconic mercenary. Traveler ran his left thumb along his stubbly chin. "Besides. I figured you'd find me when you wanted to know something."

"Well, I want to know something now. What's Milland up to?"

"The same as you. He's looking for those guns."

"And . . . ?"

"And tonight he made a mistake. He caught a roadrat and paid him off for some information. It was bad information. We went out to find Glory Boys and found roadrats instead."

"And where are the Glory Boys?"

"Beats me."

Aikers slammed the tabletop with the flat of his hand. "Damn! We've got to find out when those guns are coming through. Are you any good at scouting?"

"I get by."

"I want you to go out and scout around on your own. Find out where the Glory Boys are. Let me know."

Traveler nodded. "Sounds feasible."

"Good. Leave tonight."

Traveler slumped back in his chair. "No way. I've put in a long day, and I intended to get a little shut-eye."

"You'll do as I say."

"You don't own me, Captain. You're just renting my services. Right now, the store is closed. We open again at dawn. I'll head out then."

Aikers stared at the sleepy-eyed man before him. The squat man made a move for the pistol at his side. Before his hand made it to the holster, a knife hit the tabletop with a resounding whack. As if by magic, Traveler's hand appeared, wrapped around the knife's handle.

Traveler smiled, sending his face into a series of hard-earned lines and creases. "Time to leave the showroom, Cappy. We're removing the merchandise for the night."

Aikers slowly rose. His lower lip trembled in anger. His hand was still perched on his belt, precariously close to his pistol. Traveler knew he wouldn't use it. Aikers did, too. Someone else in the room, however, didn't.

"Throw down your gun, Aikers," boomed a voice out of the darkness.

Traveler slouched in his chair, rolled his eyes, and sighed. Aikers froze as a drunk and quite distraught Mayor James Thomas Beckman staggered out of the shadows. He clutched a positively antique Winchester 30-30 in his white-knuckled hands. Who knows what museum he raided to find it.

Beckman's eyes were the color of tequila sunrises. His speech was slurred. His upper lip was drenched with sweat. The man was in no shape to handle a shot glass, let alone a gun. "I've been waiting to get you for a long time, you sumbitch," he announced. "You've killed my little girl. My little girl."

Aikers, realizing that Beckman was out of his head with grief and alcohol, slowly made for the pistol at his side. Even at that speed, he was faster than Beckman, more in control.

Traveler, noting Aikers's slow movement, put a smile on his face and hissed to the guardsman. "Touch that gun and I'll slice your gut into an ad for zippers."

Aikers decided to leave his pistol holstered.

Traveler stood up quite casually. "Mayor Beckman. You want to do the right thing, don't you?"

The mayor stopped his forward march. "Eh?"

Traveler walked over to Aikers, slapped the chunky man's hand away from his holster, and grabbed the guardsman's pistol.

"Hey!" Aikers exclaimed.

Traveler walked toward a confused mayor. "You don't want to shoot an unarmed man, do you?" Traveler said, holding the pistol up to Beckman's face. "That's not very honorable, is it?"

Traveler called to Aikers. "Face the window."

Aikers did as he was told. Traveler smiled at the mayor. "Now, you'd even be shooting an unarmed man in the back. You couldn't do that, could you?"

Beckman, his face a portrait of bewilderment, lowered the rifle. "Well, no. I couldn't do anything like that . . . I'd be as bad as him."

The mayor's eyes glistened suddenly. He began to raise the antique to his shoulder again. "But . . . he destroyed Melissa."

By this time Traveler was more worried about this relic blowing up in his face than Beckman blowing away Aikers. He casually removed the rifle from the mayor's trembling hands before Beckman could work up a second head of steam. "Plus, if you fire this blunderbuss in here, you could wind up hitting Bess or me. You don't want the blood of innocent people on your hands, do you?"

The mayor stood, his empty hands outstretched before him. He waved them in the air helplessly. "No. No. Too many innocent people have been hurt already . . . right?"

"Right," Traveler replied. "Now, why don't you just go home."

"Right. Go home," Beckman repeated, turning and walking slowly out of the dining room and toward the lobby.

"And, Mayor," Traveler called out.

The mayor stopped in the doorway, his back toward Traveler. Traveler nodded in the mayor's direction. "You did the right thing tonight."

"I'll remember that," the mayor said feebly as he continued to shuffle into the darkness.

Aikers strutted up to Traveler. "You had no right to interfere! I could have handled it! I could have killed him!"

Traveler emptied Aikers's pistol on the floor before handing the weapon back to the piggish fellow. "Yeah. So what? Your shots would have woken up everyone in town. Before long, this place would have been swarming with armed turkeys from both your and Milland's headquarters."

Aikers's face was burning. "So?"

Traveler turned his back on the sputtering man. "So . . . like I said. I've put in a long day, and I want to get a little shut-eye."

He turned around and glared at the man. "And crowds keep me up. And when I don't get enough sleep, I get real, real cranky."

Aikers stood in the middle of the dining room, simmering. Finally, he turned and stomped out of the room. Bess stood at the snack counter and laughed softly to herself, watching Traveler slowly head out of the dining room and into the lobby. If only she was a hundred pounds lighter.

# 11

The Meat Wagon sped along the barren, burnt-out desert as the sun rose. Plumes of radiation-tinged dust arose in its wake. Traveler was excited. He had a plan. Sort of. Well, it wasn't so much a plan as an attitude. He didn't know what he was going to do, just yet, but he knew he had to do something. The stalemate in town was beginning to drive him nuts. In another day, he'd snap. And if he did snap, a lot of people would die. Maybe some that didn't have to.

Inside the wagon, he flipped on his C.B. radio. You never could tell; if there were government troops in the area, maybe they'd be communcating with their home base. And, if the troops were in as gonzoid a condition as the rest of the world, maybe they'd be using citizens band. Hell. No one else had C.B. units anymore. Only the rich and the very powerful, and the very mobile. Traveler figured that the army was all three.

Traveler hadn't been driving for twenty minutes when the C.B. started squawking, ever so faintly.

"Recon to CO. Recon to CO."

Traveler braked, turned up the radio, and listened. It had to be the Glory Boys. That jargon had gone out with the bombs. Anybody, everybody had worked hard to forget it.

The recon squad were the unlucky fools who preceded a squad or a platoon of men into an unknown area. It was the recon's responsibility to check out the enemy action. Recon gave the all clear if the area was safe. Recon teams were the ones who got blown away if the area wasn't.

"We have a clear," the point man barked over the radio. "No roadrat activity in sight."

"Roger, Bryce," a second voice replied. "We're rolling the six-by. Over."

Traveler took in the information. A six-by was a large flatbed truck with wooden slat sides and, usually, canvas tops. So, the Glory Boys were transporting their rifles in a conventional truck. He'd have to file that for future use.

Leaving the C.B. chattering, Traveler carefully got out of the Meat Wagon, and grabbing the Zeiss binoculars he'd found in one of hundreds of cars he'd searched over the years, stood up on its roof. He scanned the area 360 degrees. Not a sign of the Glory Boys.

The point man and his commander chatted on. They did everything but give Traveler their exact coordinates. As it was, Traveler reckoned they were about a day and a half to two days away from the town, depending on how fast they were moving. Traveler estimated their arrival as the night after next.

"How's the six-by holding up?" point man asked.

"Not too good," the CO answered.

Traveler climbed back into the car. Two days. He continued to listen to the two men. The point was pretty ecstatic about the lack of enemy action. Traveler smirked. The geek would be pissing in his pants if he knew how many roadrats were really roaming this area. Traveler sat attentively in the front seat, trying to take in and assimilate each fragment of information. If the six-by was in bad shape, then the Glory Boys would be using the roadways. And if they were using the highway, they'd be passing within two miles of the town.

Fireworks.

The commanding officer cautioned his point man to

81

be on the look out for crafty roadrats. "Just you keep your eyes open, Bryce. The rats know we're all double-veterans. He'll be remembering that and wanting to dust us good. You see anything that looks like an ambush, just bust some caps and head home."

The pit of Traveler's stomach did a flip-flop. Double-veteran was slang for the lowest of the low in gruntspeak. A double-vet would take a woman—enemy or not, it seldom mattered—rape her, then kill her. A platoon of double-veterans meant that all the President's men were animals—as bad or worse than the roadrats.

Traveler slumped in the front seat of the car. He shut off the radio and closed his eyes. He was alone in El Hiagura again. Scared shitless every time he heard of someone busting caps, firing a gun.

His nerves had been getting to him. There was something wrong about being down there. Even though he had been playing at this war game a long time, he couldn't help wondering what the hell he was doing so far away from home, from Roberta, from the kid.

He had been sitting in the jungle ruminating when he had heard the woman screaming. He spun around and ran toward a village nearby. A woman, no more than a girl, really—fourteen, fifteen tops—was running, naked, from a hut. She wasn't a hootchgirl. You could see that. Just a cherry kid. Her left nipple was bleeding. Her stomach was covered with teeth marks. As he watched in horror, a brown bar and hard-stripe sergeant emerged from the hut laughing. They wore shirts but no pants. They weren't Americans. They were part of the international peace-keeping force. Both carried Swedish K's. As the girl ran toward him, screaming like someone who had not only seen but experienced death, the lieutenant and the sergeant opened fire.

He had watched the bullets tear into her flesh. They burst through her frontside and whizzed by him. She was still screaming when she hit the ground . . . only not as loudly.

The two men had slapped each other on the back and had returned to the hut.

Traveler had quietly walked up to the hut, removed a grenade from his belt, pulled the pin, and lobbed it inside. The hut had blown sky-high, the two men inside. Traveler had walked away from it. The two guys probably wound up getting splashy funerals and a ton of medals for their glorious finales.

Double-veterans.

Now, a whole platoon of them, in the service of their president, was heading this way.

Something closely akin to bloodlust began to well within him. Traveler was still brooding when he noticed a cloud of smoke looming on the horizon. It wasn't smoke, exactly. It was more like dust.

Exiting the car, he climbed, once again, onto the roof. He held the binoculars to his eyes. In the distance, a few miles away, was the biggest mob of roadrats he had ever seen in his life. Three or four hundred, easy. On foot. On bike. On horseback. A few jeeps. The Chevy Impala.

The leader of the pack was a regal, skeletal man with long hair and a flowing, black beard. He reminded Traveler of a movie he had seen when he was a kid about a crazy Russian monk, Rasputin. With a woolen hat and a Cossack outfit, this rat could have passed for the mad monk's twin.

Rasputin sat stiffly on his Harley, talking with animated gestures to a glistening figure on his right. The roadrat leader was in the middle of a very important discussion, sharing opinions and confidences with someone who was obviously his second-in-command. Traveler smiled thinly as he adjusted his field glasses, focusing in on the features of the other marauder.

It was Mr. Moon.

"Well, well, well." Traveler chuckled. Moon. Once second to the mayor, then to Milland, and now, to

Rasputin. Ambition certainly figured prominently in this guy's life-style. Loyalty, apparently, did not.

Traveler replaced the glasses in the car and revved up the motor. He headed back toward town.

He had learned quite a bit during the course of his early morning outing. Now he had to figure out just how to put all this knowledge to good and drastic use.

# 12

"Lazarus!" Bellows exclaimed as Traveler entered the dusty bar. "I thought you'd be long dead by now."

"I keep coming back for more," Traveler said, slouching in a chair at a corner table.

"It's a bit early for a drink, isn't it?"

"It's never too early for a drink."

"Ha! Good one. Good one. Well, you know what they say. The best thing about being a heavy drinker is that when you wake up in the morning, you know you're going to feel better as the day goes by. A nondrinker wakes up in the morning doomed with the knowledge that *that's* the best he's going to feel alllll day."

Traveler stared at the table in front of him. The tabletop, the chair, and the floor were covered with a thin layer of grit. "Don't you ever clean this place?"

Bellows brought a shot over to the weary warrior. "Nah. It would only get dirty all over again. There's dirt everywhere. Haven't you noticed? It's in the air you breathe, the water you drink. Everywhere."

Bellows returned to the bar. Traveler downed the shooter. The place was pretty much empty. Jim Beckman sat, semiconscious, at his table, still muttering about doing the right thing and his daughter. One or two other spiritless characters sat before the bar's television set, staring at an empty screen. It had been fifteen years since the last transmission. Old habits died hard.

Traveler was lost in thought when the door to the bar swung open. Aikers and two of his guard-goons walked in. Aikers marched up to Traveler's table and took a seat, his two henchmen leaning against the door. One of the men stared at Traveler the way gluttons gaped at Twinkies.

"Saw your car out front," Aikers said in lieu of a greeting.

Traveler nodded. "Hard to miss."

"Did you find out anything?"

"Yeah. Your Glory Boys are on their way. They should be here within the week."

Traveler stopped short. Something in his mind clicked. He hated the man seated across from him. Plans within plans within plans. He had survived in combat keeping thoughts like that in his mind. He'd survive now the same way. You had to keep the enemy guessing at all times. Once they figured out your M.O., you were dead meat.

"How many of them?"

"Don't know. Couple of squads. Platoon. Hard to tell this early."

"Can we take them?"

Traveler regarded the man with the endless piece of hair wrapped around his gleaming head like a turban. What are you, kidding me? Can you take them? You're not a professional soldier, shithead. Neither are your men. The Glory Boys are honest-to-god fighting men and worse. No way they're going to let a bunch of overgrown Boy Scouts take them by surprise. They have the experience. They have the weaponry. They don't need the numbers.

Traveler smiled at the man. "Can you take them? I don't see why not."

"Great. I want you to go out again tomorrow morning. Get me their coordinates. Okay?"

"No problem." Traveler gazed at the men standing

next to the door. The tall man was still glowering. "Is one of those creeps your explosives expert?"

Aikers nodded. "Yeah. The tall one. Harvey."

Traveler smoothly took out his Colt and took aim in a single move. He fired once before anyone even realized the gun was out, hitting the tall man in the chest and sending him, screaming, into the wall. The lanky guardsman rebounded off the plaster surface and hit the wooden floor with a crash. The second man stood there blinking as the tall man writhed at his feet. A puddle of blood stained the surface of the wall.

Aikers stared, mouth agape, at Traveler.

Traveler put the gun back into its holster. "He left me a surprise package the other day," Traveler said evenly. "I don't like surprises."

# 13

When Roberta had been alive, she would fight off the blahs by setting off on shopping sprees. She'd visit the local mall and come back with clothes she didn't need, food that no one would eat, or figurines that would look idiotic on anyone's shelf.

Traveler spent the entirety of the afternoon shopping. He wandered around the town, breaking into hardware and supply stores and acquiring a few boxes full of seemingly worthless items. Coke bottles. Rags. Boxes of nails. Kerosine. Tape. Junk. He placed the boxes in the back of the Meat Wagon at the end of the day and trudged into the hotel, exhausted.

"You look like hell," Bess said as he entered the lobby.

"I feel worse."

"Dinner will be ready soon."

"Not hungry." Traveler paused before the elevators. "Mind if I use your roof?"

Bess nodded. "Got the heebie-jeebies again?"

"Yeah. A little bit. I need some space." He climbed into the elevator. Actually, he was doing pretty well considering he was constantly fleeing an overwhelming wave of claustrophobia. The only thing keeping him going was an all-consuming feeling of curiosity. Somewhere along the line he had realized that he was playing the Game in a manner he had never attempted before.

He was playing the championship version, the tournament finals.

Sooner or later this entire town was going to blow apart. Traveler realized that he was going to be around to witness the cataclysmic event. Not only that, he'd probably be the spark that would ignite the fuse. All he had to do was bide his time and stay out of trouble until the time was right.

The elevator passed the third floor and headed up toward the roof. As the lift shot by 3, Traveler experienced an odd flash of panic. In a second it had vanished.

Traveler couldn't understand just why he was hanging around this town. It wasn't a sense of justice or heroics. There was something here that would someday figure importantly in his life. He'd already discovered that Orwell was alive, or *had* been a year ago. That was more than he had discovered in fifteen years on his own. Yeah, his layover had paid off already. But he felt that there was even more knowledge to be mined in this stinkhole.

The elevator stopped on the penthouse level, and Traveler stepped outside. He was faced with an empty, cracked, and generally filthy swimming pool and the ghost of an adult hot spot. The roof of the hotel must have been a pretty swinging place for a college kid away from home for the first time a decade and a half ago.

White metal patio furniture still was arranged around the pool, although its alabaster skin was now flecked with blood-red splotches of rust. The canvas umbrellas towering above the tables were now mere skeletons, their gaily colored skins shredded by high winds and aberrant weather.

Traveler took a seat and stared at the setting sun. The sunsets had been remarkable since the war, the final illuminations of the dying day reflected and amplified by countless solid particles drifting in the air. Particles that had once been the backbone of what was laughingly known as Western civilization. Traveler stared at the firefly effect. He wondered exactly what it was tonight that was capturing his attention. A side of the Empire State Building? A hunk of the Kremlin? Part of the population of Paris?

For a moment the melodrama bubbling in the town below seemed insignificant. What did it matter who killed who? Who took over what? Who controlled what amount of firearms?

In the end the results would be the same.

Chaos.

Traveler willed his mind to shift gears. He couldn't allow himself to despair. His mind was fragile enough as it was. If he allowed himself to slide into an existential state of ennui, he'd become a zombie, no better than most of that lot down there. Traveler glanced at Aikers's headquarters and then at Milland's at the opposite end of the block.

Why was he staying here?

He laughed to himself.

Because he had no place else to go. Besides, he owed it to Hill, Orwell, and Margolin to check things out, to follow his gut instincts. After all, they had made a vow early on to watch one another's asses.

Hell, if they didn't, no one else would. That was for sure.

Traveler stared at the gathering darkness. Lightning flashes flickered in the middle of the billowing clouds forming in the distance.

Flashes of light.

His eyes focused on the sudden, violent explosions. "Incoming!"

The four of them hit the floor of the jungle. What seemed like tons of dirt and fragments zipped over their heads as the explosions blotted out their heartbeats.

"Thanks," Orwell muttered. "Would've missed that."

Orwell was in bad shape. He had jungle rot so bad on his hands that the only way he could carry his rifle was to cradle it in the crooks of his elbows like a baby. He couldn't fire it. He couldn't hold it. He could only cradle it.

They were lost, lonely, and alone, and it seemed like they'd been running around in circles for weeks. Every orifice of their bodies was misbehaving. The only way they could stop the shits was to eat the peanut butter in the C-rations they found in the food caches. That would plug them up good. They wouldn't shit again until they downed the grape juice. Drink the grape juice and you'd be looser than a Hanoi hootchgirl. Between the peanut butter and the grape juice they kept themselves pretty regular, but beyond that every other system was falling apart.

Traveler, Orwell, Hill, and Margolin began humping up a hill. They had gone four or five klicks when Traveler noticed something moving in the bushes. Without thinking, he grabbed his automatic and opened fire. He stood there, in the open, like a complete asshole, firing one round after another. By the time he was finished, he had almost turned the bush into tapioca. Hill ran over the liquefied shrub and began laughing.

"Hey, man," he said, staring at the carcass beneath it, "you just took out a very dangerous ox!"

Traveler couldn't believe it. The other men cracked up. Finally, it was Orwell, his hands and feet practically useless from the rot, who staggered over to the site and bent over the animal. He picked up a human hand from beneath it. The hand still clutched a grenade. "Yeah," he whispered. "A very dangerous fucking ox."

The four of them sat down on the hillside and shook. Storm clouds swirled above their heads. They were only in their early twenties, but they had seen more death than most people did in several lifetimes.

Hill removed his helmet, showing off a red mohawk. "Hey," he said. "We're a team, right? Let's promise to always look out for one another."

"We don't have to promise that," Margolin answered. "We already do."

91

"I don't mean just out here," Hill said, nervously. "I mean, no matter what happens, let's not forget when we go back to the World."

"What's eating you?" Traveler grunted. "You believe in what you see in all those bad movies?"

"I don't know. I mean, we're out here in nowhereland, right? Anything could happen, and no one would know. Remember all those guys who never came back from Nam? The MIA's? After a while nobody cared about them except their families. The government didn't give a shit. That was for sure. After a while even their buddies didn't seem to care. Well, after all, what could anyone do? You couldn't fight the government, right? But we have to be different. We have to fight. We have to care. We're family. We're more than family."

In another man's voice those words could have sounded desperate, but coming from Hill, they were merely a statement of fact. The four men were different. They were more than family. They would look out for one another . . . no matter what.

A roar shook the heavens.

"Incoming!"

The four men dove into the dirt.

"No." Traveler had laughed, sitting up. "Just thunder."

"Just thunder," Traveler repeated on the rooftop, the angry sky belching above his head. It would be raining soon. He'd better get inside. Even fifteen years after the big nightmare, the rain often brought down unwanted gifts to the earth's surface. Poisons that would kill slowly, gradually. Burn the crops. Mutate the animals.

Traveler stood on the roof as a gust of wind hit him full in the face. The twinge of panic he had felt in the elevator returned now. Stronger. More sustained. There was great danger present. More danger than any storm could bring. He slowly unsheathed the Gerber knife and laid it alongside him. He checked his Colt. Too noisy to play with when you're sitting between two baby armies. He took the crossbow from his back, cocked and locked it before placing it on the tabletop.

He stood for what seemed like hours, staring at the elevator leading to the pool.

Finally, the door opened.

His sixth sense had been correct.

Roadrats.

A half dozen of them.

The angry sound of metal on metal as a shot sent the chair next to him twirling dizzily sent Traveler diving toward the ground, snatching his crossbow off the table as he did so.

He executed a complete roll, aiming his weapon as he did so. He squeezed the trigger, sending the first arrow flying.

He watched the small projectile tear into the throat of the rat with the shotgun. An explosion of pink and crimson gushed from the rat's mouth as the man took a step backward for the last time.

Traveler's brain clicked off. He went into combat trance. He took his mind and placed it in a safe place, trusting his reflexes to carry him through.

His eyes took a mental snapshot. Five roadrats left. Two had maces. Two had knives. One of the rats held a shotgun. Traveler reached up, grabbed the knife from the table, and went into a second belly roll as a shotgun blast heated the air above his head.

A sliver of metal tore into his flesh. The shotgun was loaded with debris. Anything and everything the roadrats could get their hands on was being used as ammunition. This was both a plus and a minus.

On the plus side, the homegrown ammo wouldn't go very far or very accurately. On the minus side, the shot would spread like a bomb blast, tearing hell out of literally everything in front of it for the few feet it would travel.

Traveler loaded the crossbow and let another arrow fly. He was off by two feet. The arrow slashed harmlessly by the man with the gun. The roadrat took aim.

Traveler jumped to a crouching stance and launched himself at an abandoned snack stand. Hunks of wood took to the air around him as the shotgun chewed the snack bar into smaller pieces. Traveler quickly jammed another arrow into the bow and set it down as he drew the Colt. He waited two beats. He could hear the roadrats approaching. They probably thought they'd nailed him. He leaped to his feet. The man with the shotgun was only five feet away.

"Surprise," Traveler hissed, squeezing the trigger. The forty-five bucked in his hand, and the man stared at the last thing he'd ever see. The remaining four dove for cover as Traveler turned toward them. But when the hammer fell, nothing happened. Dead primer.

Traveler tossed the automatic onto a chair, and knife in hand, took on the quartet. Two maces and two knives slashed the air around him. Traveler ducked and rolled, his skin almost feeling the touch of the approaching steel.

Hand-to-hand combat affected his body the way an exposed electrical wire did normal people. Every nerve in him tingled. Energy surged from his brain to his toes.

One of the mace-wielders lurched at Traveler, swinging his studded weapon past the mercenary's torso. Traveler slashed the man across his right wrist, cutting an artery. The man howled as blood spurted from the wound. He dropped the mace. Traveler dropped the knife. Traveler picked up the mace and, spinning wildly, embedded it into the groin of an approaching knife-handler. The roadrat tried to scream as he tumbled headfirst into the empty pool. He landed with a sharp snap. That was the only sound he managed.

Traveler spun and faced his remaining two assailants. Somehow, at this point, they seemed less enthusiastic about their career choice.

The man with the mace took a deep breath and charged. His movements were pathetically lead-footed. Traveler had no problem grabbing the mace with his free hand and pulling the man past him. Traveler punched the man hard in the small of his back with his own mace. The punch accelerated the man's charge. He crashed through a table and two chairs before plunging through a guardrail and off the roof.

The roadrat was so surprised, he couldn't even manage a scream on the way down.

Traveler faced the remaining roadrat. He was no more than a boy. Eighteen years old. Blond hair. Ice-blue eyes. Traveler refused to acknowledge him as a human being. The boy screamed and charged. Traveler, still holding the roadrat's mace, swung it fiercely, catching the boy on the side of the head.

The boy stopped screaming.

The boy stopped charging.

Traveler tossed the mace onto the ground.

Taking great pains not to notice the carnage, Traveler picked up his crossbow and his Colt and replaced both in their holsters. He wiped his knife and placed it back in its sheath. He walked to the elevator and pushed the button for the third floor.

If roadrats had gotten into town for the express purpose of taking Traveler out of the picture, then there was only one person who could have engineered that.

Mr. Moon.

And, much as he would like to, there was no way that Traveler could take out Moon without taking on both Milland's army and Moon's loyal following of roadrats.

At least not today, anyway. Who knew about tomorrow?

# 14

The Meat Wagon sliced through the night, the moon above it besieged by angry clouds.

Traveler sat, tight-jawed, behind the wheel. He shouldn't have left the protection of the town. There were roadrats all around. But something inside of him had snapped. He had grown tired of the sight of other humans. He had grown tired of their smell. Most of all, he had grown tired of their actions.

Lightning exploded nearby. Thunder trembled in the distance. Heavy rain began to fall.

He gripped the steering wheel with both hands and pressed hard on the accelerator. He was wasting precious gas. Sure, the Meat Wagon could run on almost anything, but this was sure pushing the point.

What the hell. He'd rather lose fuel than what was left of his mind. As the Meat Wagon cut through the sheets of rain, Traveler reached over into his glove compartment and pulled out his one, solitary cassette tape. He lovingly placed it into the single luxury item he had built into the car, a cassette deck. He pushed the On button and rolled down the driver's window in a reckless, carefree action.

Within seconds the eerie, ethereal saxophone soundings of John Coltrane wafted out of the car and through the air. The rain seemed to caress the music, carefully allowing it safe passage. Traveler turned the volume to full, the car's Koss speakers accepting their duty with ease. The erratic, yet somehow melodic, phrasing of Coltrane eased Traveler's mangled nerves somehow.

It had a less than soothing effect on those within earshot of the wagon, however. A pack of wild dogs, hearing the sax squeal, abandoned a recent kill and left, whimpering for the safety of a burnt-out filling station. Two roadrats on patrol began babbling hysterically and headed for their already spooked horses. They drove through the mud as if the devil himself were snapping at their heels.

Gusts of wind blew sudden bursts of rain into the car. The rain cascaded down Traveler's left cheek. It wasn't healthy, but hell, what was?

The sound of the decades-old jazz made him remember things. Miss things he had long forgotten or, worse yet, had never experienced. Generic nostalgia.

Coltrane began wailing in earnest. Traveler slowed the Meat Wagon down, exhaustion sweeping over him. Since the war he had seen almost every horror a soldier could imagine, gone through every rotten situation in the book. He had done all one man could do to stave off madness and despair.

The Meat Wagon came to a stop. Traveler had a sudden flash of himself before going overseas for the first time. He was young, happy, alive. All he had wanted back then was a house, a wife to share his life with, and a kid to toss a ball to. Deep within his mangled nervous system was a human being who still wanted that.

He suddenly thought of Mayor Beckman sitting in the bar, broken.

He then saw Beckman standing bravely in the hotel dining room, his gun trained on Aikers, about to fight the good fight . . . albeit on automatic pilot. The old goat was willing to die defending the honor of his Melissa.

A peel of thunder punctuated a particularly daring solo by Coltrane.

A gust of rain spit at Traveler's face.

Traveler spun the car around and headed back toward the town. What the hell. He might as well save Beckman's daughter. He had nothing else planned for the evening.

The Meat Wagon sped toward the beleaguered city with a vengeance, living echoes of heartfelt jazz trailing behind.

# 15

He stood in the darkness, a killing machine. The ride back had only served to heighten his sense of outrage. He was a man with a mission now. He would rescue Beckman's daughter and kill every single guardsman in Aikers's enclave if necessary.

Aikers's headquarters sat, serenely, at one end of the town's deserted main street; a grammar school converted into a fortress. The structure was three stories high and, built in the late 1940s, was filled with latrine-green colored hallways and drab, overhead lights—the kind of lights that made the healthiest of men seem jaundiced in their sickly glow.

Traveler walked to the back of the building and, unsheathing his knife, jimmied open the rear door. He replaced his knife, grinning wolfishly. National guardsmen were not known for their military smarts. Even during peacetime the most noteworthy aspect of their warlike status was the great shine they managed to produce on their boots.

The moon was breaking through the clouds as Traveler eased open the metal door. He entered into an area that must have once been the school cafeteria but now served as a storage area of some sort.

Lockers filled with what Traveler assumed to be ammunition stood, unguarded, next to rows of rifles in various states of disrepair.

The moonlight serving as his lone source of illumination as it filtered through the mesh-wire-lined windows, Traveler edged his way through the room and walked into a corridor.

He stared down the green hallway. The walls were barren but for a few gory photos of Jesus Christ in what appeared to be a tribute to the concept of pain. He tried to imagine the school filled with kids taught by priests or nuns. Most likely nuns. He wondered what they had done during civil defense drills. He wondered if they had ever considered that their lives might really be shattered by nuclear bombs.

The nuns probably had the kids line up facing a wall reciting the rosary. Idiocy. But, then again, that was about as good a defense as anything the U.S. government had cooked up.

Traveler stopped and stood before a picture of the crucifixion. It didn't affect him one way or the other. He'd seen worse. Hell, he'd *done* worse. He stared at the painting. At least *his* agony ended after a few hours. For the survivors of planet Earth, the agony would go on for decades upon decades.

He sheathed his knife and removed the crossbow from across his back. He loaded the bow and took to the stairs, climbing silently to the third floor. That's where Aikers's office was, and that's where Traveler had felt the pain strongest . . . the pain of a young woman.

The hour was late. Most of the guardsmen were fast asleep in classrooms converted to fairly nice sleeping quarters, each housing only three or four men. Traveler reckoned that Aikers had less than a hundred men in his direct employ. It struck him as odd that an entire town could be cowed by so few.

Then again, Traveler had never been good at power games. He was better at shooting than talking.

His body went rigid. A guard was approaching. Traveler eased open the door to one of the sleeping rooms. Four guardsmen snored blissfully as the fully armed mercenary stood, holding his breath, next to the portal. One of Aikers's men passed by outside, carrying a rifle as casually as most kids carried a baseball bat.

Sloppy.

Very sloppy.

Traveler waited until the guard had finished his tour of the floor before returning to the hall and resuming his hunt for Melissa. He stayed close to the wall in an attempt to pick up stronger emotional sensations. The sensation of fear began jangling in the back of his head. With each subsequent step the aura of fear and pain increased. The brutalized girl was nearby. A second wave of emotion began filtering in to his senses as well. It was slow and heavy and possessed a sleepy, semiconscious feel. Someone was either very drunk, very drugged, or very near death.

Traveler clutched his knife as he walked softly down the hall. The pain grew stronger as he grew closer to its source. He stopped suddenly outside a wooden door riddled with bullet holes. He thought his forehead would explode from the agony within. This was it. No doubt about it.

He opened the door slowly. He was not prepared for what he saw. Four naked guardsmen lay in a stupor. Their bodies were sprawled on a plush, black pile carpet. Various empty vials and bottles were strewn across the room. They muttered and grunted in their sleep.

In the center of the room, resting on a series of pillows, was a beautiful, naked woman. Raven-haired and heavily made-up, the woman rocked her right leg back and forth. She was giggling, emitting half words in between bursts of lascivious laughter. Traveler noted that her large, gray eyes were feline. Her lips were wide and sensuous, almost obscenely so. She was in her early twenties.

Something was wrong here.

The woman kept on giggling. "You want more? Come on, honey. Been waiting for you. Been wanting it."

101

Traveler stood at the door. He shook his head back and forth suddenly, as if under the impact of a left hook. He had to try to sort out the emotions here. The drowsiness hitting him in ripples was emanating from the guardsmen. They were higher than most successful NASA launches.

But sure as hell the pain wasn't arising from the woman before him.

"Ms. Beckman?" he ventured.

Silence.

"Melissa?"

The woman lolled about on the pillows. "Yeah. Yeah. Come on. Come on."

Traveler placed his crossbow on the carpet and walked over to the woman. She stared up at him.

"Who are you?" she mumbled. "Do I know you, honey?"

"I'm a friend."

The girl seemed to consider this fact for a moment, filtering it through a drug-induced fog. "Well," she said, smiling, "all right, then. Come on."

She reached up suddenly and grabbed his crotch.

The move both pained and surprised him.

He thrust her hand aside. He was puzzled. He was still being assaulted by a steady mantra of pain, but he was sure it wasn't Melissa's. He grew more confused every moment he remained.

"I've come to take you away from here," he said, bending over the girl.

She slid a hand up the inside of his leg. "You're kidding me." She laughed softly. "Take me away? What for?"

"Well," Traveler stammered. "Because of all this!" He pointed to the naked men and the empty bottles.

Melissa struggled into sitting position, her ample breasts flopping this way and that. She emitted a braying laugh. It defined the word pornographic quite nicely.

102

"All this? All this? Darling, I love all this. We're family here."

Traveler blinked, her words really not registering.

Melissa continued laughing. "They use me. I use them. We're living high here. We party till we drop. Then we get a little fresh meat and party some more."

"But they kidnapped you!"

Melissa was slowly coming out of her stupor.

"Old news, honey. Zeke and the boys take good care of me, you know. We have enough supplies and goodies to see us through another war. And when we run low, Zeke just sends out some guys and they come back with some more!"

Traveler's mouth dropped open with a crack.

Melissa continued to caress his leg. "And you know what? When Zeke takes over, I'm going to be his woman. His queen. Yeah. His queen."

Traveler backed away from the woman. "But the pain . . . I sense great pain here."

"Oh, a witchman, eh?" Melissa lurched to her feet. "Well, to put your mind at ease, you're right. Like I said, I was kidnapped and got used to it. But Allison is newer. Just here a couple of months. She fights us. We fight back. But good."

Melissa walked over to a small recess in the wall, something that must have been used as a clothes closet at one time. Melissa slid open the door. "And, behind door number 2 we have Allison! Taa-daa."

Inside, a young girl with short blond hair was tied on the floor. She was in her mid-teens. Her body was a mass of cuts, bruises, and cigarette burns. "Pain." Melissa snorted. "She'll get used to it. Right, honey?"

Melissa bent down and gave one of the naked blonde's breasts a hard tweak.

Traveler growled and grabbed the black-haired woman by her mane. He pulled her away from the girl and tossed her behind him. He heard her hit the wall with a thud and a half-audible curse.

103

Traveler reached into the closet and gently pulled the whimpering young girl to her feet. Her blue eyes blazed with fright.

Traveler faked a thin smile. It didn't do much to quell either her fear or his nausea. "It will be okay," he heard himself say. "We'll get you out of here." He began to lift the girl up into his arms.

"Put her down," he heard Melissa slur from behind him. "She's mine. Zeke promised me. First she'd be ours, then she'd be mine."

He heard a familiar sound of plastic on steel. His crossbow had just been loaded.

He eased Allison down on the carpeted floor and slowly turned around. Melissa held the crossbow in her sweaty hands. "You can't come in here and just take our toys away. We all need our toys."

The woman was so far gone that she would have no second thoughts about using the bow on him . . . or the girl.

His eyes clouded for a moment. He was in the jungle. He was staring at death. Without hesitation he palmed his knife and let it fly. Melissa was opening her mouth to utter yet another threat when the blade entered. She squeezed the trigger of the crossbow as the blade emerged from the back of her skull. The arrow whistled by Traveler's shoulder, embedding itself in the closet door behind.

Traveler glanced down at the sobbing girl. His mind took refuge as the killing machine, outraged at the atrocity, went into high gear. He pulled the arrow from the door and crossed the room. He reached down to the spot where Melissa lay, gagging and writhing, and pulled out the knife. She was dead. It would just take her body a few moments to realize it.

Eyes glazed, he walked silently across the room, stopping over each one of the sleeping guardsmen as he did so. He saw the kids killed by guerrillas and left on the jungle roadsides. He saw the women raped and

104

mutilated. He saw the town square of this little town covered with bodies.

Stooping over each one of the guardsmen, he clamped a strong right hand over their noses and mouths and slit each one of their throats with his Gerber's razor-edge. He was careful to leap out of the way of the small founts of blood as they erupted. It was hard keeping your clothes clean these days.

When all four men were bathed in their own life force, he stepped back to the closet. He repacked his crossbow.

The violence in him exorcised, he opened the closet door and pulled out a bathrobe. He gently bent over the girl. He cut her bonds, removed the tape from her mouth, and gingerly clothed her in the robe.

"It will be all right," he assured her.

The girl stared at the blood-soaked room and, then, fearfully at Traveler. He looked tenderly into her blue eyes. He would have cried if that were possible. It wasn't, so he just shrugged. "I'm sorry."

He scooped the girl up in his arms and exited the room, leaving the five revelers behind forever. Carrying the girl down the stairway and toward the back exit, he felt strange, then stranger.

All at once he felt both noble and foolish, heroic and hideous. He slipped out the back door. The girl's face was bathed in the rich glow of the moonlight. She was sleeping. He heaved a sigh. He supposed he shouldn't be troubled by the events of the evening. He had gone into the compound expecting to rescue a damsel in distress. He had done just that.

He guessed it didn't matter if it was the wrong one or not.

# 16

When Traveler entered the hotel lobby, a mute Allison still cradled in his arms, he found Bess waiting for him a few feet from the front entrance. There was a look of alarm on the portly woman's face.

"In the back. Quickly. Quickly," she whispered.

She ignored the presence of the girl until Traveler had followed her into the safety of a small office located off the dining room. "Who's the doorprize?" she asked.

"Her name is Allison," Traveler replied. He gently placed the girl on a Naugahyde sofa, the kind that a low-cost shrink would use on a patient. "She was a prisoner at Aikers's."

The girl curled into fetal position on the sofa's surface. Her left arm twisted itself upward, revealing a scar across her wrist that was not that old. Bess carried a blanket over to the sofa and spread it over the shivering girl. She grabbed the girl's thin wrist in her own hand and gazed at the scar. It was at that point that Traveler noticed Bess had a similar, more faded mark on her own right wrist. Bess realized Traveler was staring at her. "I wasn't always this fat," she said, straightening. "You do what you have to in order to survive."

"Can you hide her here for a while?" Traveler asked.

"I have a choice?" Bess smirked. "I suppose this means that Aikers will be spouting flames tomorrow."

"Probably," Traveler acknowledged.

"Well," said Bess, once again ignoring the dazed girl, "that should just add a little extra pizazz to the fireworks."

Traveler shot her an inquisitive glance.

Bess heaved a sigh. "You have our simian chief of police, Henry Harrison, upstairs with four of his chimps."

"I don't get it."

"They came in a couple of hours ago looking for you. I said you had gone out. They asked to see your room. Not without a warrant, I told 'em. I mean, we may be on our way back to the Stone Age around here, but I still have rules, right? Well, much to my chagrin, one of his guys pulls out a warrant. It's not worth the paper it's printed on, but it's just what I asked for. I couldn't stop them.

"They went right up. They seemed to know what they would find there. I sure as hell didn't."

Traveler eased himself into a straight-backed chair next to Allison. The blue-eyed blond girl stared vacantly at the wall. "What did they find?"

"Jim Beckman . . . with a hole in his chest big enough to put your fist through."

Traveler exhaled slowly. The irony of the situation did not amuse him in the least. While he was out trying to save Beckman's innocent Melissa, who turned out to be as bad as any of the weekend warriors gone wrong, Beckman was being offered up as a sacrificial lamb in some political ceremony. "Any idea how Beckman got there?"

Bess shook her head. "It beats me. I never saw him come in. I had a couple of guardsmen in the dining room earlier tonight. They came in for one of my surprise omelets. A few of Milland's men were in here, too."

"Was Moon with them?"

"Come to think of it, yeah."

Traveler sighed. "Well, I suppose I have to ride this one out."

Bess looked at the girl on the couch. "Don't worry

about the door prize here. I'll keep her hidden until . . ."

"It won't be for long," Traveler vowed.

He got up from the chair, patting Allison on an exposed leg. "Stay put, squirt."

He walked over to the office's small desk and removed his crossbow, placing it on the green blotter before him. "Hold this for me, will you? I don't want them getting their hands on it. It would be hard to replace. Is there a back door near here?"

"Next to the kitchen."

"I'll go out the back way and walk around to the lobby. You can make a fuss when I enter the lobby. We'll take it from there."

He paused for a moment. "Do they still have jails here?"

Bess smiled thinly. "If they find one for you, I'll bake you a cake with a file in it."

Traveler and the red-haired woman faced each other. "Go easy with Harrison," she cautioned. "He's a real gorilla. An ex-biker who's here because it's comfortable. He's not your typical prewar cop."

Traveler left the office and walked to a door at the rear of the dining room kitchen. He stepped outside. The moon shone serenely above. A crisp breeze ruffled his close-cropped hair. He took a deep breath. The air smelled bad. Maybe it was just that he wanted it that way. He exhaled and walked to the front of the hotel.

He strode through the entrance. Bess was at the front desk.

"Well, hello there," she said in a loud voice. "Just getting in, are we? Late night?" She made a sour face and nodded toward the stairway.

Traveler caught the sight of a shadow on the landing. Probably a geek on the first floor. He grunted and headed for the elevator. When the shadow realized no one was climbing the stairs, it disappeared.

Leaving the elevator car on the third floor, Traveler

walked down a deserted hallway until he came to the door of his room. He opened the door quickly. A truncheon was hurtling toward the back of his head by the time he had swung the door halfway open. It occurred to him that he couldn't make his arrest seem too easy.

He spun around and faced his assailant. His mind tripped back twenty years to martial arts training. He was a vicious young student tossed out in the real world again. He lashed out with his right foot. His toe was aimed lethally, with a precision that would have done his instructor, Sergeant Lueh, proud. The tip of his foot smacked into the soft part of the cop's abdomen directly below the sternum. It slammed upward with a terrible intensity, plowing forward over the liver and through the diaphragm. It crushed the right ventricle of the man's heart. The man uttered one gurgling scream before Traveler caught the upright corpse by the left wrist and swung it in a wide arc.

A second policeman was rushing toward him. Traveler used the body like Thor used his hammer, striking the approaching cop across the torso and sending him smacking against a wall. He let the corpse go. The dead policeman sailed across the room and out the window with a tinkling of glass. He heard the body hit the ground below with one, final thump.

A gun clicked behind him. Traveler froze.

He turned around meekly. Police Chief Henry Harrison stood there, holding a Magnum, his face a fiery red. The man really did look like a simian; pushed-in nose, overhanging brow, broad jawline. He resembled a poster from *Planet of the Apes*.

"Traveler?" He snorted.

"Present." Traveler smiled.

"I'm here to arrest you for the murder of James Beckman."

The chief prodded Traveler toward his blood-soaked bed. A sheet had been pulled over something bulky and drippy. One of Harrison's remaining men yanked the sheet away. Beckman was sprawled on his back, his open eyes still contemplating the ceiling. His chest had been blasted away.

Traveler turned to the police chief. "I don't suppose it would help if I said that I didn't do this."

Harrison grinned at the mercenary. "You used to have the right to remain silent, you used to have . . ."

Traveler walked up to the sweating oaf. "Isn't the chief of police suppose to uphold what passes for law and order?"

Harrison stopped reciting his version of the Miranda. "He is," he replied.

Traveler nodded. "What are you holding up other than your pants?"

Something smashed into the back of his head. He staggered to his knees. He could take anything they could give him, he thought. They wouldn't kill him outright. He knew that. Moon must have needed him as a scapegoat of some kind. Moon was buying time with Traveler's arrest. He must have guessed just how much Traveler knew and just how big a threat he could be. With Traveler safely tucked away in jail, Moon and Rasputin the roadrat could go about setting up the entire town for a big fall.

No, Traveler wasn't about to be killed just now . . . and that thought kept Traveler sane.

His sanity slipped a bit, however, when he saw through the throbbing pain one of Harrison's men approach him with a syringe.

"This will keep him quiet for a while," a voice thundered from above.

"No!" his mind screamed.

With his nervous system so hypersensitive, a drug of any kind could drive him right over the edge. Destroy his mind.

He tried to lash out at the officer with the needle. He couldn't. The needle entered his skin with an explosion of suffering. He lost consciousness almost immediately. He slipped through time. His body belonged to the police now.

His mind was up for grabs.

# 17

Captain Peter Vallone had deserted him. He knew that as soon as he had walked into the trap. He'd been point man that day, routine stuff. He'd seen the enemy and radio'd the info back to Vallone. Vallone had led his men out of there and left Traveler behind as a booby prize.

And, now, he was in a prison. A hooch, really. Just a straw hut in the middle of nowhere. He was tied tightly. He couldn't have escaped if he had wanted to. He was blindfolded and curled, in a fetal position, on the damp earth floor.

They took off his blindfold when they came in. Three of them. One of them had a metal bar, three feet long or so. They asked him questions. He gave no answers. The little man with the metal bar inserted the bar in the space below his armpit and twisted it. His arm bent at an ungodly angle. He screamed in pain. The barman was an expert. For the next hour or so, he twisted every one of Traveler's limbs to the breaking point, both figuratively and literally.

He never actually broke a bone, of course, but he found more ways to generate pain through bizarre angles than anyone Traveler had ever encountered before.

After an hour they left Traveler, groaning on the ground. They muttered something about later. Traveler groveled in the dirt, his hands tied behind him. With his fingers he searched for anything in the grit that was sharp. A piece of glass. A stone. A rusty nail. Anything. Eventually, he found what he needed. A sliver of metal, perhaps left over from a grenade. This village had been fought over before. He jammed his wrists against that metal sliver and pushed his bonds over its edge relentlessly. Eventually, he wore through his bonds and most of his skin. He gave the ropes around his wrists a sharp tug. They came apart. He then undid his feet and sat on the floor of the hooch.

He waited.

After a small eternity the men entered again. Traveler leaped at them, grabbing the metal bar. Growling like a beast, he swung the metal bar through space, hitting the men over and over and over again. He didn't know how long he had bludgeoned them, but when he regained his senses, he was standing in a mess of blood and debris. There was nothing recognizably human in the hut. And that included him.

He bent over a battered skull. "Nobody keeps me," he wheezed, wild-eyed. "Nobody."

He ran out of the hooch and into the jungle, a soldier wearing only his dog tags and his shorts and carrying a bloody slab of metal. It wasn't long before Orwell, Margolin, and Hill found him. Even in the jungle, that sort of sight attracts attention.

He nearly wound up in a UN peace-keeping stockade shortly after his rescue, however. It seemed that he wouldn't give up his metal bar. He kept on trying to use it on his commander, Captain Vallone. It took his three buddies six hours to coax the weapon away from him.

Traveler doubled over, feeling a fiery shellburst of pain inside his stomach.

"Again!"

His mind shifted gears. It was back-in-the-saddle time again. He was in prison. In Tendran. Harrison was doing his daily aerobics on his belly. He drifted out of the present and into a netherworld of pain and dreams. He saw Melissa float in front of him, naked and laughing. She smiled at him. She had no teeth. She erupted in a whirlwind of flames. Allison screamed from a nearby mountain. Vultures were circling her. The mountain shook. It slowly took the form of Bess. Bess yelled at Traveler to wake up. Traveler felt his strength returning. He could take anything they gave him.

Compartmentalize. Isolate the pain. Get in touch with the different parts of your body, acknowledge their presence, shut out the offending zones until they're needed.

He struggled to gain control. His efforts were hampered by the presence of the drug. He could feel it roaring through his system. Each heartbeat seemed to echo like a kettledrum. Someone was still pounding his stomach. He wasn't strong enough to open his eyes and see their faces.

He remained in limbo. Why bother to waken? If he remained physically out of it, the cops might get tired of their game. No sense in torturing an animal when the animal wasn't responding to the pain, right? Where's the fun in that?

He could feel the throbbing in his midsection ease off as the mind took over. When the next blast of pain arrived, his body fielded it, spreading the pain around. His stomach muscles disappeared, leaving the zone free and easy. The pain gradually dissipated.

"Hold it. Hold it," a voice announced. "You might as well stop."

"How come?"

"He's out. He can't feel anything."

"One last time? For good measure?"

"Forget it. Let him be."

Traveler's body was allowed to hit the ground. He felt himself make contact with something solid. He gradually allowed certain areas of his body to come to life. He stank of blood, sweat and urine. He had obviously

114

lost control but that mattered less to him than how long he had been under.

He opened one eye. He was in a jail cell. A window above him told him that it was morning. The sun was up but not yet high or hot. He figured he'd been out for four hours. Maybe five.

He opened his other eye. Moon sat before him. Seeing Traveler's eyes flutter, Moon picked the prisoner up and tossed him, roughly, onto the cell's cot.

"They're going to nail you for Beckman's death." Moon grinned, sweat glistening off his bald pate. "I'll make sure of it. And while everyone is fussing with you . . ."

Traveler's lips were dry, caked with blood. "You'll try for the guns and slip the roadrats into town."

Moon lashed out at Traveler with the back of his hand, catching the mercenary across the cheek. Traveler was so numb that he hardly felt it.

"Your bravura show is stupid, do you know that?" Moon ranted, hitting Traveler over and over. "Stupid! Stupid! Stupid! You think you can just ride into this town and upset the plans I've worked on so carefully for so many months? Stupid!"

Moon paused for a moment. Traveler shook his head clear. "I get the picture, Moon."

Moon stepped back and grinned at the bloodied warrior. "But not as big an idiot as Milland and Aikers. They stand out in their field. The two of them have butted heads again and again. Neither of them has ever dared make the first move because they're both paralyzed with fear. Neither one of them will ever take the initiative. Do you know why?"

"They're stupid?"

"Cowards. Neither one of them can see that the real source of power in this world lies beyond these city walls. Nomads! Those wandering tribes out there. They are the future. They know this land. They know where life can exist, where death awaits. Align yourself with those tribes, and you inherit a communal knowledge; knowledge that is an integral part of the rebuilding process."

"You're going to rebuild America?"

"Not personally, no. But I can have a piece of it, don't you see? Gain the trust of those nomads, start an alliance, and you can take over this town. Any town. Any road. Milland would never chance such a move. . . . But I would. I decided to try. I put a white flag on my car and drove into the middle of their camp. It turns out that the leader of the biggest rat pack is a very civilized man. A survivalist.

"We struck up a bargain. If I kept my ears open and alerted him to any Glory Boy activity in the area, he'd take out the troops, and we'd split the guns. We'd both benefit that way. I am in a perfect position here at the fortress to monitor local activity, and he's just the sort of fellow who can act on my information. I will be the brains behind these pilferings, and he will provide the muscle. He's promised to loan me a squad of roadrat enforcers to rule this town after we get the guns."

"And you believe him?"

"Of course. Why shouldn't I?"

Traveler rolled his eyes. "But nobody has figured out where the guns are, have they?"

"No."

Traveler grinned.

Moon was interested. "Do you know when the guns will arrive?"

"Not only that, but where."

"Tell me!"

"What's in it for me?"

"Your life."

"Not enough. I'll get out of this alive one way or the other."

Moon stared at him incredulously. "You are an overconfident sonofabitch." He thought for a moment. "All right. First, I'll get you out. Then, I'll see that you get a town of your own to rule. With those guns we can spread out over half of this state."

Traveler tried to look like he was seriously considering the offer. "All right. Deal. The guns will be passing by the town tonight. The Glory Boys won't take the regular surface road, though. It's too close to the city. They'll be off road about ten miles west of town. If I were you, I'd get all my little roadrat friends assembled before it's time and just wait it out."

Moon chuckled to himself and moved toward the cell door. "That's just what I'll do . . . sucker. Thanks for the tip. I'll drink a toast to your scouting abilities after your funeral."

"And I thought you were such an honest guy," Traveler said, mockingly.

Moon bent over him and raised a hand to strike the mercenary, but before Moon could hazard any further movement, Traveler reached out with his left hand and pulled Moon down to the cot. They stared at each other nose to nose. Silently and swiftly Traveler hit the man with a kidney punch. Once. Twice. Moon screamed. Three times. Moon gagged and spit blood. Traveler released his grasp, allowing the tall man to roll onto the floor. "You've been a bad boy, Moon, and someone had to punish you."

"I'll see you dead for that," Moon moaned. He called to a guard. A cop arrived and led him, limping from loss of breath, out of the cell. Traveler slowly got to his feet. Removing his pants, he stumbled over to a wash basin and rinsed them out, using a half bar of soap.

He stood lost in thought during the scrub. Moon, Aikers, and Milland had just given him all the ingredients for a massive coup. He chuckled out loud. And, by putting him in here, they'd handed him a perfect pulpit to stage it from. When he was finished washing his trousers, he put them back on sopping wet. He got onto the floor and began doing sit-ups. He pushed the

117

drug further back into his blood stream. He yanked himself back into alertness.

By the time he'd reached fifty sit-ups, he had the whole plan figured out. With a little luck he could play hero after all . . . and not screw up.

"Guard," he yelled.

A pimply-faced cop showed up.

"Can you get a message to Bess at the hotel for me?"

"Maybe."

"If you fetch her over here, I can guarantee you free meals at her place." He didn't know if that was a promise or a death sentence.

The kid considered the offer. "And what if I don't?"

Traveler put on his fiercest, hard-assed sneer. "Then I can promise you I'll be chewing on your guts by nightfall."

The kid didn't bother to ask how Traveler planned on carrying out his threat—which was just as well considering that Traveler didn't quite know himself. Thinking hard on the offer and concluding that food, no matter how bad, was more appetizing than a nasty death, the kid scurried off.

A half hour later the towering figure of Bess loomed outside the jail cell. She and Traveler immediately plunged into a tense, terse conversation.

"You're out of your head," Bess concluded after a few minutes.

"You have any better ideas?" Traveler countered.

Bess stood, silent. "No." Her dour expression gradually gave way to a broad smile. "Well, on the plus side, the whole thing is so crazy that it just might work."

"It has to work," Traveler summed up, "or else we're all dead meat. You, me, and this whole goddamned town."

Bess turned to leave.

"Do you have everything down exactly?" Traveler called out after her.

118

"Do you take me for an idiot?" she snapped. "You want Milland here in a half hour. Aikers in an hour."

"Right. And make sure they know that. . . ?"

"That you have information that will ensure their sovereign rule over this great and vast kingdom."

Traveler shook his head ruefully. "You have a smart mouth, you know that?"

"I practice." With that Bess was off, waddling down the corridor and toward the front office of the jail.

Traveler sat down on the edge of his cot, cradling his chin in his calloused hands. Finally, all the years of military training with their combat and strategy sessions were going to pay off for something he believed in. People. He heaved a colossal sigh. It was time to end the stalemate and arrange a showdown.

# 18

Milland paced around Traveler's cell, his hands clasped behind his back, his distinguished face pushed into a parody of concern. "I know you're a mercenary. A soldier of fortune. A killer. That's why I hired you. But I can't believe you'd murder James Beckman for no reason."

"I didn't." Traveler shrugged.

"Then who did?" Milland queried. The tall man stopped pacing and stood before a bare wall.

Traveler leaned back on his cot and regarded the man coolly. Plans within plans within plans. "Aikers did."

Milland seemed to consider that answer for a moment. While his face remained impassive, his eyes flickered with dim understanding. Possible. Possible.

Traveler took in the man's reaction before playing his trump card. "Of course, he had a little help."

"Help?"

"Your man Moon."

Milland staggered as if he'd taken a blow. "What?" His distinguished facade collapsed utterly. "What you're telling me is preposterous!"

"I have no reason to lie to you, Milland," Traveler said. "No reason at all. Look. Moon is out for himself in this mess. He wants a bigger slice of the pie. Right now, he figures that Aikers has a better chance of retrieving those guns than you do. After all, Aikers *does* have *some* military experience. Moon has been sucking up to Aikers since I arrived. In fact, Moon has been playing footsie with Aikers's men for the last couple of nights on patrol."

"Impossible."

"Really? Has he been hanging around your headquarters in the evening lately?"

"Well, no. . . ."

"Taking off by himself for long periods of time?"

Milland was silent.

"Well, there you go."

Milland's forehead formed a stairway of creases. Traveler could tell that the angular man was putting two and two together and not liking the sum total at all. Milland's face suddenly lit up. In a show of desperate optimism he said, "Last night! Last night he told me he was going to the hotel for dinner. Some of my own men saw him there!"

"Yeah. And I bet those same men spotted a few of Aikers's guardsmen hanging around there as well."

Milland hesitated. "Well, yes. . . ."

"And Beckman was found dead in that hotel last night, right?"

Milland nodded gravely.

Traveler stood up. "Look. The fact is I saw Moon outside the city with one of Aikers's patrols the night before last scouting for the Glory Boys. I didn't say anything to you because for all I knew he was out spying on your behalf. From the look on your face, though, I can see that he wasn't."

Milland was beginning to brood. Traveler was beginning to enjoy himself. "I'm not asking you to believe me outright, but tonight, why don't you have your best men ready. Follow Moon when he leaves town. I guarantee that he'll lead you directly to that shipment of guns."

Milland suddenly became animated. "The guns are arriving tonight?"

Traveler nodded, motioning to the cell walls around him. "Why else to you think I'm in here? With me knowing about Moon *and* the gun shipment I . . ."

"Yes," Milland interjected, "Moon *would* want to see to it that you couldn't interfere, wouldn't he? Since he couldn't kill you, framing you for a murder would certainly keep you out of the picture, wouldn't it? Well, I'm ready for his trickery. Rest assured that you will be released from this cell by nightfall, Traveler. And I shall see to it that you are rewarded handsomely for this information."

Traveler nodded solemnly. "Just passing it along to you is reward enough . . . sir."

Milland called for the young guard. The kid opened the cell door, allowing Milland to step into the corridor. Before making a final exit, Milland turned and, with a true politican's hindsight, announced; "You know, I've had suspicions about Moon all along. He was one of Beckman's men before I arrived. His most trusted aide. Did you know that?"

Traveler feigned surprise.

Milland nodded vigorously. "Oh, yes. A treacherous man, this Moon. Treacherous."

Milland strutted out of the corridor, a master of retroactive precognition.

Traveler sat down on the cot and whistled between his teeth. The effects of the police chief's drugs were almost completely gone. He began to feel the confines of the prison walls. His body began to tremble. He began to shake. He shut his eyes and fought off the attack. He had to keep it all together. Just a few hours more and he'd be on the outside. Just a few more hours and all the fuses would be lit.

He kept his eyes closed and compartmentalized. When he opened them some fifteen minutes later, the slimy, stocky figure of Zeke Aikers had replaced the tall, lanky presence of Milland.

"What do you want?" Aikers growled from outside the cell.

"I thought you might want to chat?"

"About what?"

"About how Milland is going to wipe you out tonight."

Aikers assumed the position of a chimpanzee deep in thought. Grasping the bars to Traveler's cell with his pudgy hands, he eyeballed the mercenary. "What the hell are you talking about?"

"You wanted me to spy on Milland, right?"

"Yeah, so?"

"Well, I found out too much. Milland had one of his men spying on me."

"Who?"

"Moon."

"That asshole?"

"That asshole killed Beckman last night."

"What for?"

"To have me tossed in jail. To keep me from talking to you."

Aikers shook his head back and forth. The man was badly confused. It didn't take much. "I don't understand."

"They're setting up a smoke screen, Aikers. They're pulling stuff off left and right that you don't know about."

"Milland and Moon? They're not that smart."

"Oh, yes they are. They got me for killing Beckman, right? That was supposed to shut me up. But if they didn't get me for old man Beckman, they would have gotten me for Melissa Beckman's murder and the killings of your men."

Aikers stiffened. "No one was supposed to know about that."

Traveler smiled. "You take care of your own, right? It's only because you didn't go around ranting and raving to the police that I'm here on one count of murder and not five or six."

Aikers was clenching and unclenching his fist in a slow but steady rhythm. "How did you know about Melissa?"

"Milland was here a half hour ago to gloat over me. He was bragging about it."

"That sonofabitch!" Aikers barked. "I'll kill him."

Traveler got up off the cot and held out a restraining hand toward the prison bars. "I've got a better idea."

Aikers allowed himself to be stalled.

Traveler smiled ever so slightly. "Those guns you were after?"

"What of them?"

"They arrive tonight. Milland knows that. He'll be sending out some of his men to get them. Follow Milland and you'll have your guns."

Aikers's eyebrows seemed to connect at this point. He screwed up his Cro-Magnon countenance into something vaguely resembling concentration. "How can I believe that?"

"You don't have to. But think about this. I know about the guns. I know about Melissa. I know about your dead buddies. I know too much, Aikers. I was caught working for you, and here I sit. Framed. If he thought he could kill me without losing half his troops, he would have done that."

"Yeah," Aikers muttered. "Yeah. It sort of makes sense. Damn that Milland! I'll catch his ass tonight and grind it into the ground."

Traveler sat down on the cot. "I could do you some good out there tonight."

"Don't worry about a thing," Aikers said from between parted lips. "You'll be out of here by nightfall. I promise."

Traveler placed his hands behind his head and leaned back on the cot. He was on a roll. Might as well try one last maneuver. "Oh, and another thing . . ."

Aikers froze.

"That girl Milland snatched last night? Allison?"

Aikers reacted as if he'd been hit with an anvil. "A-Allison?"

"He killed her," Traveler concluded.

Aikers roared and stormed down the corridor. On the way out, he silently took a swing at the wall. He sent his fist through it. He pulled out his hand and marched off, leaving a trail of blood and plaster behind him.

Traveler leaned back on his cot and started to hum. Suddenly, the cell didn't feel so confining.

# 19

Nightfall.

A humid breeze hummed through the deserted streets of the town, stirring up dry heaps of dust. Somewhere in the darkness, beyond the confines of the city, wild dogs fought. Howling. Snapping. Tearing. Feeding.

In the tacky hotel dining room, Traveler attempted a meal. Attacking Bess's psuedo-food with a fork, Traveler suppressed a shudder. The stay in the jail cell hadn't done him any good. The drugs had slowed his system down even further. He would need all his strength to pull off the plans he had for this evening.

A strange tingling hovered at the base of his spine, a mixture of exhilaration and dread. It was a feeling he had dealt with countless times before: before a major battle, before the birth of his son, before leaving the veterans hospital.

Bess walked over to the table. She was carrying Traveler's crossbow. "Thought you might be needing this."

Traveler's fork attempted to keep pace with the lique-fied goop running around his plate. "You keep it for the time being. I've packed everything I'll need."

Bess sat down next to the mercenary, regarding him in silence for a moment. "You're nuts. You know that?"

"I'm a victim of my environment."

Bess snorted through her nose. The stillness in the

room was broken by the Brobdingnagian footsteps of Terrance Bellows as he lumbered through the lobby. The barrel-chested barkeep was sweating, half from the humidity, half from dread. He was carrying an M-16 rifle, a memento from a war fought long ago over a long-forgotten hot spot in Southeast Asia.

He plopped into a chair next to Traveler and Bess. "I don't know about this. I don't know about this at all."

Traveler stared at the food on his plate. "Me neither."

Bellows shook his head mournfully. "You're nuts, you know that?"

"That seems to be the popular consensus."

Bellows motioned to the front door behind him. "The town feels like it's going to pop."

Traveler smiled thinly. "Not pop. Explode."

Bellows stared at Bess in amazement. "He's enjoying this!"

Bess laughed ruefully. Traveler continued to regard his plate with a sense of morbid interest. "Remember what you said about this town needing a hero, Bess?"

"Yeah?"

"You were wrong. . . ."

The woman's face fell. Traveler waited a beat before adding, "You need a whole townful of them."

Bess slapped Traveler on the back. "I knew you were a fighter."

"If he wasn't," Bellows smirked, "he wouldn't be eating your food."

"How's the girl?" Traveler asked.

"Allison? She'll be all right. She's still in shock, I think. She must have been worked over pretty good by Aikers."

Traveler pulled a piece of bone out of his food and held it up before Bess's eyes. "I could have sworn I boned the jello," she said sweetly.

Traveler focused his attention on the black barkeep. "How many firearms did you get?"

"All I could find. Half a dozen rifles, half a dozen

127

sidearms, and the extras out of your truck. Not as many as I hoped."

"They'll be enough for you to get those men out of your jail at the college."

"I'm not too sure about that, Lazarus," Bellows replied. "There are too many guards up there."

"Tonight there won't be," Traveler said. "Most of Aikers's and Milland's best men will be on a trip."

"Where are they going?" Bess asked.

"Nowhere. But they don't know that yet."

"What did you do to get those boys movin'?" Bellows inquired.

"I told them just enough to get their attention."

"Greed city?" Bess grinned.

"You got it."

"I still don't understand," Bellows said.

"You don't have to," Traveler replied, getting to his feet. "In about an hour this town is going to be left unguarded, or close to it. You'll have about a half hour to get those men out of jail. Bellows, you call the shots. You're regular army. How many men have you got?"

"Counting Bess?"

"I'm all woman, buster," Bess said sternly.

Traveler rolled his eyes. "Not counting Bess."

"Four." Bellows sighed. "Mostly rummies. I've had them drying out for a few hours."

"Then you and Bess are going to have to throw your weight around the most."

Bess was not amused. "Any other wisecracks?"

Traveler smiled thinly. "Come out to the Meat Wagon with me and watch the fun."

Bess and Bellows exchanged puzzled glances and followed Traveler out into the parking lot next to the hotel. Traveler sat in the driver's seat, leaving the door opened. Bess and the barkeep leaned on the side of the mini-van.

The way Traveler figured it, Moon would join his roadrat buddies as they attempted to intercept the Glory

128

Boys. Thanks to Traveler, however, the roadrats wouldn't come near the caravan. When Moon left for his rendezvous, Milland would be in pursuit, figuring that his two-timing crony would lead him straight to the guns. Aikers, in turn, would follow Milland, thinking that it was Milland who knew where the Glory Boys would be. One big happy parade. Everyone who was anyone in town would wind up gate-crashing the roadrat powwow.

Traveler smiled to himself.

It was the little things in life that gave him the most pleasure.

And these were the mighty leaders who threatened to kill him a few days ago.

Bad judgment on their part.

Traveler sat up slightly. "Here we go," he whispered.

Bess and Bellows watched, amazed, as the festivities began. Moon silently strode down the block, climbed into a jeep, and quietly pulled out of town. Five minutes later close to one hundred of Milland's men left the city, in cars, trucks and a few on motorcycles. Milland himself brought up the rear of his party, riding in a bulletproof limo—the kind once used by presidents and visiting dignitaries when the worst thing that they had to fear was a lone assassin's bullet. Traveler ran a thumb across his lower lip. Milland may have been slimy, but he traveled in style.

The dust had barely settled behind Milland's motorcade when Aikers, looking a bit like a modern-day Attila the Hun, led a band of seven dozen guardsmen toward the barricades.

Most of his men were stuffed into a dozen or so badly mangled early '60s convertibles. Gas-guzzlers, first class. A dozen or so of the guardsmen rode on horseback.

"What a sorry looking bunch," Bellows grunted as Aikers, sitting in a massive motorcycle sidecar, paraded by with his driver.

Traveler watched the ragtag group exit. He revved up the engine of the Meat Wagon. "I have to do a little

129

shopping before I head out," he told his companions. "Have the men wait near the front barricade after you spring them."

He eased the car into drive and pulled away. Bess and Bellows watched the Meat Wagon turn down a side street.

"The man is definitely nuts," Bellows commented.

"Yeah," Bess said, nodding, "but we're helping him."

"We probably have some sort of vitamin deficiency or something," Bellows said sadly. "I've seen that crap you serve in your restaurant. It retards mental growth."

The two walked slowly down the street toward Bellows's bar. "Like your dog food is a lot healthier, right?" Bess grimaced.

In the Meat Wagon, Traveler casually drove to the rear of Aikers's schoolhouse-compound. He parked outside the back exit. He waited a moment. There was no reaction from within.

He casually drew his Colt and jacked a round into the chamber. He stepped out of the car and walked cautiously up to the door. He knocked. No one answered. He eased the door open and stepped inside. He glanced about the locker area where the guardsmen's ammunition was stored. There was no one present. Traveler figured that he wouldn't need too many rounds. Tonight, he hoped, he'd be more an observer than a participant. Still, it didn't pay to take chances. He began rifling through the lockers. It wasn't as if he was actually *stealing* the stuff. After all, Aikers did *owe* him something for a few days work.

He picked up a few boxes of .45 ACP for the Colt and a bag of clips for the rifles and tucked them under his right arm. As he strolled back toward the door, a tall, droopy-eyed guardsman strode into the room, holding his rifle, poised.

"What are you doing?" he demanded.

"Leaving," Traveler said, not breaking stride.

130

"Oh," the guardsman replied. "What's that in your hand?"

"Which hand?"

"I can see that's a gun!" the guardsman said. "I want to know what else you got."

"Ammunition. I'm taking it to Captain Aikers."

"Oh. Okay. Have a nice day."

Traveler shook his head in amazement and left the compound. Some humans hadn't advanced as far from their one-celled ancestors as many scientists believed. He reached inside the wagon and tossed the ammunition into the front seat. Climbing behind the wheel, he revved up the motor and sped off.

Outside the confines of the town, Traveler roared along the highway, the moon keeping track of his every move. Traveler could easily make out the dust trails left by the two groups ahead of him. He sighed and hit the accelerator, sending the mini-van hurtling off road. He felt a little like God must have while watching the participants line up for Custer's Last Stand.

A sharp pang on his left shoulder brought him out of his mental reverie. He scratched the itch vehemently.

He reckoned that God never had to contend with fleas on such momentous occasions.

# 20

Traveler sat atop the Meat Wagon on the hillside, bathed in darkness. He had driven like a maniac to get to the site quickly, but he figured that the gas expenditure would be worth it. This was one show he did not want to miss.

Traveler watched.

Waited.

Below him, Moon, his bald head gleaming in the starlight, was doing some heavy explaining to the hook-nosed leader of the roadrats. Moon must have gotten word to the nomad chief about the Glory Boys' where-abouts shortly after Traveler fed him the bait. Right about now, Moon was probably beginning to worry about the validity of Traveler's information.

Rasputin the roadrat was waving his arms wildly in the air. Although Traveler couldn't actually hear the conversation, he pretty much imagined the content of the dialogue. Rasputin was asking where the government caravan was. He was probably wondering how Moon could be so sure that the guns would, indeed, be passing this way.

Moon, in an attempt to cover up just how chancy his information was, was presumably doing a big number on how he came about the information, making his source seem very mysterious and very important. As the two men gesticulated at each other, Traveler scanned the rest of the scene.

The roadrat assembly was fairly large, with at least two hundred half-assed warriors in attendance. Most of them looked the worse for wear, their clothes a sorry array of rags, their skin a patchwork of radiation burns and plague scars.

They were fairly well armed, however, about half of them carrying automatic weapons of some sort. The rest brandished an assortment of rifles, spears, longbows, and clubs that would make a museum proud. They possessed a few dozen cars, a small herd of horses, and twenty or thirty well-worn choppers. Traveler regarded their primitive appearance with a solid sense of irony. The world had made it past the year 2,000 A.D., but half of its inhabitants looked like they would be comfortable vying for living space with dinosaurs.

Traveler turned his attention to the other side of the hill. A small army of oversized fireflies were bouncing merrily along the roadway. Headlights. Lots of them. The first wave was slowly undulating toward the site.

Traveler slid off the auto and sat on his haunches in the dirt. He had his Armalite AR-180 at his side, just in case. He didn't really want to use it, though. Not just yet.

Moon was still in animated conversation with the leader of the tribe when Milland's men came barreling around the hill. Milland's people were probably just as surprised at seeing the roadrats as the rats were at seeing Milland and company.

After all, Milland was looking for the Glory Boys and their guns.

Then again, so were the roadrats.

Traveler laughed out loud. "Surprise!"

Before the full shock could set in, the two masses of men reacted instinctively. A single shot was fired. Then another. Then another. Before long, both armies were

133

charging each other for no apparent reason but for the fact that they existed.

Traveler stood and, retrieving a pair of field glasses from the van, watched the unfolding drama with a keen sense of anticipation. Rasputin the roadrat, sizing up the situation immediately and suspecting foul play, pulled out a handgun and, holding it to a paralyzed Mr. Moon's ear, blew the top half of the bush-league politico's head off. Moon's body stood there for a split second, his hands outstretched before him, pleading for a reprieve even after his brains had mingled with the dust and grit beneath the boots of the charging roadrat troops.

Rasputin jumped on a Harley and, raising his rifle high, charged into the fray. He was immediately run over by convertible full of Milland's men, squashed like a bug. So much for drama.

Milland's men showed their combat experience, coolly picking off the nomads with their rifles. They displayed the kind of ease shown at a carnival shooting gallery. The choppers flopped over like wooden ducks on an eternal treadmill. What Milland's men failed to notice while they pursued their two-wheeled targets was that the roadrats on foot were lining up, Roman infantry style, with their longbows raised.

One of Milland's convertibles hurtled into their line of fire, and the bowmen reacted with deadly accuracy. Six of Milland's men were immediately impaled by dozens of long, lethal shafts. The car tires burst into a chorus of hisses as the arrows tore into the rubber. Blood and flesh spattered on the seatcovers as the silent death sliced through the riflemen. The convertible slowed down before sputtering to a stop.

Milland's bulletproof limousine, reacting to the slaughter, whirled around and headed directly for the rows of archers. The roadrats, seeing the oncoming auto, scattered. Ten of the slower runners, however, were mowed down by the careening car. As the limo fishtailed around for another pass, Traveler saw that the car's massive front grille now had a disembodied arm, still clutching a longbow, impaled on it.

He tried to imagine Milland in the backseat barking orders in a demented but dignified manner. The arm slid off the grille and fell in the path of the limo's churning wheels. Semisolid matter splattered out from beneath the tires.

As the carnage spread from the roadway to the adjoining roadside, Traveler backed up to the Meat Wagon. He clicked on the C.B. and fished around for any and all signs of the approaching Glory Boys.

"Mattson on point," he heard a voice say faintly. "We have a town up ahead. Things look pretty dead. We have a clear. Over."

Traveler flicked off the radio. He'd have to double back pretty quickly in order to get the job done.

He leaned up against the van for one last look at the insanity below. As he watched Milland's minions and the roadrat renegades clash, he saw a billowing cloud of dust emerge from around the hillside. Aikers and his men charged out of nowhere.

Traveler eagerly raised the field glasses to his eyes, trying to catch the expression on Aikers's face when the fat guardsman realized that he had just ridden into an intramural war that had nothing at all to do with either guns or Glory Boys.

Traveler found Aikers at once and focused on the sweaty captain. Clutching his sidecar with one hand, Aikers began waving at his men behind him to slow down. The men, misinterpreting his hand gesture as a sign to charge, rode their horses and jalopies jubilantly into the skirmish. The cavalry met Milland's motorcyclists head on, with most of the horses spooking immediately. A gust of wind blew Aikers's one long strand of hair askew, uncurling it and giving the swarthy man a Mongol look. Aikers fell back into the sidecar as a spear sliced through his driver, sending the goggled

135

guardsman flying backwards over the machine. The motorcycle and sidecar zoomed, out of control, off the roadside and into the night.

Traveler watched it all with a morbid sense of fascination. He felt as if he had been transported back to one of the Roman circuses, wherein gladiators battled to the death for the amusement of the masses. Two hundred feet below him countless men slaughtered one another with every type of weapon imaginable. He was suddenly overwhelmed by the amount of humanity nearby. It was oppressive.

It was too much for him to take.

His knees suddenly gave way. A look of horror shot across his face. Not now. Please, not now. He struggled to regain his footing. He reached out to grab the handle of the Meat Wagon but clawed the air instead. The events of the last few days, the claustrophobia created by the town, the effects of the drugs and the beatings, descended upon him without warning.

His body began to tremble, then to shake. He tumbled backwards, his spine undulating wildly on the dirt surface of the hill. His eyes rolled back. Saliva spurted from his mouth.

Not now. Pease, not now. He was too close.

His vision blurred. His teeth began to slam up and down, up and down. With a Herculean effort, he reached out with his left hand and felt around the ground for a twig. Finding one, he jammed it between his teeth. If this kept up, he'd bite his tongue off.

He shook. He cursed. He moaned. He ranted. He rolled back and forth, over and over in the dirt. Damn it. Slow down. Compartmentalize. Everything inside him was exploding. The gunshots from below thundered in his ears, hurting his brain, causing his eyes to tear. The stench of blood and flesh filled his nostrils, sending his stomach into spasms of near nausea. The light of the heavens blinded him. The feel of the dirt below his body sent shards of pain up and down his spine.

He rolled on his side, his entire body convulsing like a fish tossed from a lake onto a skillet. He flip-flopped toward the car. Perhaps he had one chance to pull himself out of it. His arms searing under the effects of imaginary flames, he reached out toward the abandoned rifle leaning against the car. He slithered toward it. His fingers aching, his mind a mass of muddled images, he grabbed the rifle, placed the butt on his stomach, and rolled onto his back.

Pointing the rifle skywards, he began firing round after round after round. The gunshots, their rythmic sound echoing through the night, gave his mind a pattern, a mantra to latch onto. The steady recoil motion hammering into his midsection gave him a physical experience to center his nerve endings around. Gradually, the imaginary pains subsided. The roar of the battle became secondary to the steady belching of the weapon in his hand. The pain pricks, the heat, the burning caused by his brain, disappeared, superceded by the gun butt's relentless movement.

When he felt sure the fit had subsided, he stopped squeezing the trigger. He lay there for a short eternity, bathed in sweat, staring into the heavens. His lungs fought for air. He allowed the gun to fall to his side. He slowly got to his feet. He glanced down the hillside. The battle, now with only half the amount of participants as before, still raged. Traveler shook his head clear, threw the rifle into the front of the car, slid behind the wheel of the Meat Wagon, and started back toward town.

He hadn't had the neurotoxin hit him that hard in over a year. He had to watch himself. He wasn't superhuman. He silently cursed himself for risking his own life to play town hero.

Speeding back toward the city, he leaned his head out of the driver's window and spit a dozen splinters as big as his thumbnail out of his mouth.

# 21

In its heyday, Murdoch College had been a quiet but distinguished college, one of the most exclusive in the state. Before Armageddon, rosy-cheeked co-eds and blow-dried frat boys cavorted on its lawns, made love in its dorm rooms and, if conditions were favorable, actually learned a new fact or two in its classrooms.

After the war the campus became the town's gathering place. A symbol of the old normalcy, it suddenly served as a power base, a place to plan for the future. Then, Aikers and Milland arrived. The campus was transformed into a death camp of sorts, a setting where people were either butchered or broken.

The college's spacious cafeteria had been converted into the twenty-first century equivalent of a dungeon. Devoid of light or sanitary conditions, the room was now stuffed with weakened, dejected townsmen, ranging in age from thirty to sixty. They spent their waking hours staring at each other and their sleeping hours running headlong into nightmares.

Shortly after the mass incarceration, many of the younger men tried to escape. They were shot. Gradually, the escape attempts trickled off. Months passed. The weaker prisoners died. The older and infirm were "disappeared" by the guards.

All of the men would have been killed but for the power it gave the two intruding armies. The power of

138

fear. An occupied prison was both a show of strength and a source of fear. As long as they held these men, the town would never strike back. Since both sides valued the prisoners, warriors from each army stood guard, side by side.

On this night a half dozen men, three from Aikers's camp, three from Milland's, marched back and forth in front of the cafeteria.

They were somewhat surprised when Bess waddled out of the darkness carrying a Heckler and Koch HK91 assault rifle.

"Howdy, boys." She smiled.

"Halt!" cried one gangly guardsman. "Identify yourself."

"Why sure, honey. I'm Bess Armstrong, owner and operator of the town's finest—and only—hotel."

"Oh, yeah," the guardsman said. "I knew that." His five peers gathered at his side.

Bess turned to her right and waved a second figure out of the shadows. The towering figure of Terrance Bellows, also armed, strode forward.

"Halt!" the guard began yammering again.

"Oh, just relax, honey," Bess said. "This is my good friend, Terrance Bellows. He's the bartender and manager of Leone's. You know, the joint where you guys all guzzle up every day?"

"Oh, yeah," the guardsman replied. "I knew that."

"Great. Great." Bess smiled. Bellows and Bess stood before the half dozen guards, cradling their rifles. The guards were puzzled. The pair in front of them didn't move.

Silence.

"Uh," the guardsman began, "I'm not sure I understand why you're here."

"Oh, sorry," Bess said. "We're here to get those men in there out of jail."

Bellows nodded affirmatively. "That's right."

139

The six guards tensed somewhat. The leader smirked openly. "Right. Just you two?"

Bellows shook his head from side to side. "No, sir. We have four drunks behind us."

A short guard began cackling. "You two and four drunks are going to spring all those prisoners?"

Bess smiled sweetly. "That's the plan, hon."

The wiry guardsman raised his rifle, pointing it at Bess and Bellows, then raised his voice, "I appreciate all you people coming out tonight, but it's getting late and we're getting cranky. So, fat stuff and friend, put the rifles down on the ground where we can see them, turn around, and then, get the fuck out of here, okay?"

Bess and Bellows faced each other and shrugged. They silently placed their rifles in the dirt at their feet.

The short guard began cackling again. "How did you ever expect to take over this prison by yourself? Oh, sorry. With four drunks?"

Bess and Bellows smiled and dove onto the ground. "We gave them guns," Bellows shouted. "Big guns."

Four grizzled old men leaped from the shadows behind the pair and opened fire on the guards with shotguns. They pumped round after round over Bess's and Bellows's heads. The six guards were practically ripped apart, their bodies spinning around under the impact of literally hundreds of double-ought buckshot like marionettes with their wires crossed.

The four winos stopped firing only when they ran out of ammunition. It was obvious that these guards were not going to do anything but bleed. Bellows helped Bess to her feet.

"Thanks, boys." Bess nodded at the quartet.

She waddled past the guards, glancing at their bullet-riddled bodies. "And the moral of this story, children, is: There are good drunks, and there are mean drunks. It pays to know the difference."

Bellows double-timed it past her, hitting the locked

cafeteria door with one of his huge shoulders. The door flew off the hinges without much trouble.

Bess called into the darkened room. "Up and at 'em, babies. It's freedom time."

# 22

Glory Boys were almost all crazy.

That was common knowledge. They were a lot more dangerous than roadrats. Unlike the traveling bands of nomads, the Glory Boys had no sense of clan or tribe or loyalty. They were rapists, killers, and worse, united loosely under one leader and allowed to do any damn thing they wanted under the banner of patriotism.

Traveler didn't like Glory Boys much. He had been proud of his soldiering and wasn't appreciative of what the new army had mutated into.

He had seen a pack of these vermin descend on a small encampment of roadrats once. They had butched the men first. Then, they tortured and killed the women. They left the children for last. Some of the men assaulted the kids before they shot them. He remembered one big, bearded soldier who dangled a piece of gum in front of a wild-eyed little boy. Spearmint gum. After about five minutes of taunting the boy, the Glory trooper let the stick of gum drop into the dirt. The kid dove for the gum. The Glory Boy opened fire. Later, Traveler had counted twenty holes in the kid. He had burned the bodies and kept on moving.

He sat, hunched in the rock formation, still shaking off the effects of the fit. His body still seemed to be on fire. Behind him the town sat serene.

He hoped that Bess and Bellows were hard at work

142

right about now. If not, his whole plan could go down the toilet within the hour.

Before him stretched an endless highway. All he could do now was wait and watch and hope. Sooner or later, if his sixth sense was in working order, the shipment of guns would pass right under his nose. And when it did, he'd be ready.

The crackling of walkie-talkies caused his back to arch. The point man was nearby. Traveler scrambled down the small cliffside to the right of the roadway. He ducked behind a large boulder and waited. Two Glory Boys, clad in uniforms that seemed a cross between army infantry and cat burglar, trudged up the road. They wore standard camouflage pants and standard army boots but wore cowboy hats instead of helmets and long-sleeved black shirts. Both of them had jaws square enough to crack walnuts and clean-shaven heads.

Traveler wished he had his crossbow. A silent, quick, clean kill would be the best. He cradled his AR-180 in his arms. It would have to do.

One of the two point men was speaking into his walkie-talkie. "We're still clear. Over."

The walkie-talkie hissed and burped a garbled sentence back as a reply. The point man grunted back and replaced the walkie-talkie in a side holster.

"You think we'll have time to stop at that town?" the Glory Boy on the right shoulder of the road asked his companion.

"I sure hope so," the other one grunted. "We haven't had any fun in a long time."

"Remember that ratcamp last month?" the first point man chortled.

"Do I ever." The second grinned.

Something in the back of Traveler's mind clicked into gear. His mind went numb. His jaw tightened, and he jumped out into the middle of the road directly in front of the two Glory Boys.

They didn't even have time to say "What the. . . ?"

Traveler was tired of all these fools, and right now seemed like a good time to show them how tired. The fool with the radio took the Gerber in the throat—hard. As his buddy tried to untangle the strap on his Uzi and bring the gun to bear, Traveler had time to pull the big knife loose and put it in the second man's chest before he got his jaw off the ground. As soon as he caught his breath, Traveler dragged the bodies into the underbrush and set himself up to watch the parade.

He walked over to the Meat Wagon, hidden behind a massive pile of boulders. He pulled out the packages he had pilfered from the town's stores and prepared to be creative. The nice thing about living on your own after a nuclear war was that you learned very quickly how to make do.

Traveler sat on the ground and, in the light provided by a flashlight, spread out the junk before him. As he did so, a wild dog, perhaps attracted by the smell of fresh meat, trotted up to the area. He stood within ten feet of Traveler, bared his fangs, and growled menacingly. Traveler stared at the dog and did the same.

Apparently, Traveler was very convincing. The dog ceased growling, cocked its head to one side as if wondering how the world had fallen into such a confused state, turned, and trotted off, its tail at half-mast.

Traveler took a half dozen Coke bottles out of a sack and spread them out in front of him along with a few boxes of nails, blasting caps, some kerosine, a few wads of *plastique* he'd been saving for a rainy day, a ball of string, a roll of tape, a pile of rags, and assorted debris. Filling the Coke bottles with kerosine and wadding them with long strips of rags, he made a half dozen fairly primitive Molotov cocktails.

He then emptied the boxes of nails onto the roadway. Taking the plastic explosive, he wadded it into a series of squares. Taking a pencil from the pile of random junk, he pressed a round hole through the center of each *plastique* square. He packed the nails tightly together on long strips of tape. He then wrapped the strips of nails around the explosive rectangles.

Taking pieces of string, he dipped them in kerosine, creating a series of fuses. He placed a blasting cap at the end of each fuse. By the light afforded by the strong flashlight, he inserted the fuses, blasting cap side first, into the plastic explosives, taping them in securely.

Within a half hour he had made six nicely packed nail grenades—charges powerful enough to frag a few dozen men.

Making sure the Meat Wagon was safely out of sight— he'd have to abandon it for a few hours or so, and he didn't want a roadrat to heist it—Traveler moved behind a rock formation on the side of the roadway and waited.

# 23

The tall, gangly guardsman sitting sentry in the storeroom at Aikers's compound had seen a lot since his arrival in the town, but nothing had prepared him for what awaited at the back door. Answering a timid knock, he swung the portal open. In the moonlight stood a fat woman holding a rifle. She was flanked by two old men with no teeth. They both had shotguns trained on him. Behind the two codgers was a mob of pasty-faced men with sunken cheeks, dark-rimmed eyes, and matted hair.

The guardsman's mouth flapped open and shut helplessly. No sound came out of his mouth. The fat woman smiled and casually removed the rifle from his hands. "That's a good boy," she cooed as she waddled past him into the storeroom.

The two old men each took one of his arms and led him into a chair. They deposited him in the seat firmly.

"Now." The fat woman smiled. "How many more guardsmen buddies do you have upstairs?"

The sentry's mouth couldn't stop moving. Still, no words emerged.

"Maybe I should blow his head off," one of the old men offered.

"No, no, William," the fat woman admonished. "He's just surprised, aren't you?"

The guardsman nodded yes.

"It's not that he's trying to be uncooperative, it's just that he's in shock, isn't it?"

Another affirmative nod.

The fat woman leaned over him. "Well, get over the shock, junior, because William and Roger would love to use their shotguns on you, and the fellows behind them are itching to do something with their hands. Now, once more. How many men upstairs?"

"Eight."

"Do you have an intercom set up here?"

"Yes, ma'am."

"Good. Call them down."

"Down here?"

"Now."

The sentry walked over to a small box stuck haphazardly onto a wall next to a locker. He pressed a button. "Hank? It's Steve. You and the boys had better come down here right away."

"Trouble?"

"I'm not sure."

"We're on our way, Stevie."

Bess gently walked over to the boy, took him by the arm, and led him back to the chair. "Good. Now just relax. No one will get hurt if everyone just relaxes."

She handed the guardsman's rifle to one of the freed prisoners. "Don't shoot unless you have to, hon."

Within minutes, the sound of footsteps could be heard approaching the room. Bess, the prisoner, and the two rummies trained their guns on the entranceway. Eight guardsmen, pistols drawn, tumbled into the room, led by a tall, blond man.

"Far enough, boys," Bess said.

The eight men, their momentum carrying them to the center of the storeroom, gaped at the sight before them. They found themselves encircled by weirdos and zombies.

"Throw down your weapons, and everything will be just fine," Bess advised.

The guardsmen hesitated.

"Should I blow their heads off?" the eager rummy asked.

"William, please!" Bess snapped.

The guardsmen gradually realized the extent of their helplessness and threw down their guns. The tall blond, however, seemed unduly tense.

"Fine," Bess commented. "Now, take off your pants."

The guards exchanged bewildered glances.

Bess shrugged. "Take off your pants and toss them in the center of the room."

The guards did as they were told.

"Fine. Now we're all going to take a little walk to the college campus, and some of these men here will show you your new home. It's an old cafeteria. It needs a little fixing up . . . but I'm sure you'll like it. Oh, yes, and before we all move, again, please don't try anything rude. My companions are very irritable, okay. Now, let's march, boys."

Before the guardsmen could move toward the exit door, the tall blond pulled a knife from a scabbard secreted below his left arm. He didn't get the chance to use it. The mob of former prisoners in the room simply dove on the man. His screams were muffled by the angry yells of the townsmen. Bess looked on in muted horror as a dozen of the newly freed inmates literally tore the guardsman to pieces before her eyes.

She turned to the gangly sentry. "See? I told you they were itching to do something with their hands."

The sentry looked around him, dumbfounded.

Bess heaved a colossal sigh. "Okay, men. We're off to the campus . . . unless anyone else has a death wish."

The remaining guards exchanged panicked looks and scurried out the door in their boxer shorts.

# 24

For a downright upright southern boy like Jimmy Maltin, the sight of Terrance Bellows towering above him was the culmination of every nightmarish story he had ever heard down home. There was Jimmy, not yet thirty years old and Mister Milland's trusted third-in-command, sprawled at the feet of someone who was twice his size, twice his weight, and black. Adding to Jimmy's misery was the fact that Bellows also was pointing a very large rifle at his Adam's apple.

"Now," Bellows was saying, "let's chat."

Jimmy's first reaction was to tell this big mother off, but the close proximity of the rifle barrel's cold steel to his own warm flesh encouraged newfound discretion and courtesy.

"W-what do you want to know?"

"How many men has Milland left here?"

Jimmy hesitated. He looked between the black man's legs. Waiting at the door were two old men brandishing shotguns and a dozen or so emaciated males. Jimmy decided to cooperate. This was the type of audience you didn't want to antagonize.

"There are ten men, including me."

"Fine," Bellows grunted. "Now, stand up."

Jimmy stood.

"Move over to the desk and call them on the intercom. Tell them that Milland needs reinforcements immediately."

"Yes, sir," Jimmy replied, almost choking on the word *sir*. He parroted Bellows's instructions into the intercom. The man on the other end didn't seem surprised.

Within five minutes Bellows had all of Milland's men in tow. "Fine," he said to the newly gathered group. "Now, we're all going to hike over to the college campus where you boys will be staying for a little while. Okay?"

Milland's men were not about to argue.

"Sure."

"Fine."

"Sounds great to me."

Jimmy fumed at the burly black man. Who the hell did he think he was, giving orders like that? Jimmy casually patted the derringer strapped under his long-sleeved shirt. The small handgun was attached to his left hand on a spring lever device. All Jimmy had to do was extend his arm straight out and the gun would pop into his outstretched hand. If he could position himself behind Bellows, he could take the big man's head off with no problem, get his gun, and go to town.

Bellows marched the ten men into the middle of the main street. They headed off toward the campus. En route, they passed another grouping of ill-clad men on the way back. The second troupe was led by the fat woman from the hotel. Jimmy didn't know exactly what was going down, but if he was destined to die in this stinkhole, then he'd take these townies out. He'd die like a soldier.

Jimmy began to slow his pace.

The two juicers with the shotguns and most of the zombie types passed him by, keeping pace with the rest of Milland's men. Jimmy figured that only the black man and a few of the zombies were behind him. The black man was talking to one of the men.

"It's going to be a whole new ball game from now on," the nigger was saying.

Jimmy grinned. Yeah. It was going to be a whole new ball game, all right, cause you'll be one dead sonofabitch, boy. Jimmy figured he could just whirl around and catch the oaf with his head bent to one side deep in conversation when he fired. He allowed the big man to chat for a few more seconds before he made his move.

Pivoting on his right foot, he twirled and faced Bellows, his left arm stuck straight out. As the derringer slid into his hand, a look of shock registered on Jimmy's face. The big black man was taken totally by surprise. Jimmy could kill him. No problem. Just behind the big black man, however, was the fat woman from the hotel. She must have stopped in the middle of the street as soon as she had walked by. She had her rifle already trained on Jimmy.

Before Jimmy could squeeze the derringer in the palm of his hand, he saw the barrel of her rifle emit a small flick of light. Something slammed into his chest with a splat. He felt his arms jerk up in the air and felt the breath leave his body in a sudden, violent *whooosh*. Jimmy Maltin tumbled onto the street directly in front of a still-shaken Terrance Bellows.

Bess shook her head and walked up to the barkeep. Bellows stared at the twitching boy before him. "How did you know?" he muttered.

"I didn't," Bess said matter-of-factly, "but he looked too cool for a guy wearing a long-sleeved shirt in ninety-degree weather. Struck me as kind of odd, you know? I just figured I'd monitor the situation for a while. Then I saw him slow down. Didn't take a military strategist to size up the rest, honey."

Bellows looked at the fat redhead with a newfound sense of awe and respect. "You saved my life!"

Bess reached over and tweaked Bellows's cheek. "You

151

men are such helpless darlings." She then turned and strolled back in the opposite direction. "Lock those guys up and then come back to the barricades. We'll pass out whatever arms we can scrounge up and wait for Traveler. I have a feeling the fireworks are only just beginning."

# 25

He sat on the side of the cracked macadam roadway and shivered. He had no idea why he was doing this. He wasn't a hero. He wasn't an avenging angel. He was just a man . . . a fairly screwed-up man. His body was a mass of short-circuited nerves, and his mind was a feverish conflict of terms. He chuckled to himself. If things weren't so pathetic, they'd be funny.

Traveler's exercise in self-pity was interrupted by a movement a few miles down the road. Headlights bounced serenely in the blackness afforded by night. Traveler raised his field glasses to his eyes.

The convoy was approaching.

He muttered a curse under his breath. The parade was bigger than he had expected it to be. A dozen jeeps. Four men in each. Six jeeps positioned in the vanguard of the convoy, six bringing up the rear. Two dozen men riding shotgun, so to speak, on horseback. They flanked the jeeps on the outer sides of the road. Traveler had to force himself not to laugh. It was Audie Murphy's army meeting John Wayne's westerns.

Traveler peered through the glasses. In the middle of it all was his prize. A truck. A single, solitary truck packed with guns and ammunition. With that shipment any local maverick could become a warlord. Or, conversely, any targeted town could drive off any would-be warrior.

Two Glory Boys were in the cab of the truck. Driver and guard. Traveler figured that there might be from two to four men in the rear of the vehicle with the arms. He couldn't tell because the cargo had been covered by a tentlike canopy stretching over the truck's frame.

Traveler watched the convoy snake forward.

There was something wrong with the setup. It almost seemed too easy. The hairs on his neck arched suddenly. Of course. If the guns were as valuable as everyone said, then President Frayling would surely have more men attached to the convoy than this. That meant there was a second wave of soldiers nearby, probably bringing up the rear a mile or so behind. Traveler figured it was a variation of the old search and destroy missions the army used in Nam and most of the southeast border wars. Send a platoon into a heavy enemy area and let them get ambushed. Once the enemy was out in the open, the platoon under attack would call in an air strike.

In this case there was probably a cavalry just waiting to ride to the rescue. Not only would they get the guns through, they'd get rid of a few of Frayling's enemies en route as well.

The only thought that kept Traveler from getting up and walking away from the whole deal was that the second wave of soldiers would probably be keeping their eyes and ears peeled for groups of would-be marauders . . . not lone mercenaries.

After all, only a total madman would try to single-handedly take on a convoy this size on his own.

So, there you had it. Traveler sighed and slung his Heckler and Koch HK91 over his shoulder. He had enough rounds on him to slice a couple of jeeps in two with this baby if he had to. If he was going to go out in the proverbial blaze of glory, he'd make sure that his spark cremated as many of these glory-seeking fools as possible.

Traveler trotted off down the road and nestled himself in a rock formation some fifteen feet above the road, just past a bend. He could hear the jeep engines purring cheerfully. The clomp, clomp, clomp of hooves on asphalt echoed in his ear.

He reached inside his pants pocket and produced a battered pocket lighter.

Taking the HK91 and placing it at his feet, he lined up the Molotovs behind a large rock. He then lit the rag fuses. The half dozen bottles blazed behind the rock. Traveler held his breath. The convoy began to pass by.

"Showtime!" he wheezed, picking up the first bottle and tossing it over his head. Without looking up, he grabbed each of the bottles and tossed them down onto the road as quickly as possible, before any startled infantryman could see exactly where they were coming from.

He peeked over a boulder to see exactly what damage he was doing. The first Molotov hit a cavalryman, shattering on his back. Both the rider and his mount exploded in flame. The man and the horse screeched as the liquid inferno spread rapidly. The air was suddenly filled with the acrid odor of charred meat.

Traveler heard the startled cries of the men as he ducked under the cover of the rocks. He grabbed his rifle and the clip-filled butt-pack and ran to a second rocky location some twenty feet down road from the first.

A jeep burst into flames and left the road. It hit a ditch and overturned, rolling three, four, five times before crunching to a halt. Five of the cavalrymen rode over to the injured vehicle. As they approached it, the vehicle exploded into a gigantic fireball, cremating the approaching soldiers immediately.

Another jeep caught a Molotov. The four passengers dove out of their flaming vehicle, themselves afire. They rolled, screaming on the ground, attempting to put out the flames. Unfortunately, they squirmed on a part of the road directly in front of the rest of the convoy. Their screams subsided as the jeeps and truck moved forward, undaunted by any obstacles before them, human or otherwise.

The entire front section of the convoy was in chaos. The driver of the truck carrying the guns attempted to accelerate but found that impossible, his path blocked by the careening jeeps. The Glory Boys were panicking. They hadn't expected anything like this.

Two more jeeps ignited, the conflagration sending their occupants twisting and turning into space and, ultimately, onto the ground and under the hooves of the stampeding horses.

As the convoy tried to regroup, attempting to logically assess just what had occurred during the last ten seconds, Traveler unzipped the butt-pack and removed the nail grenades. He lit and tossed. Lit and tossed. Lit and tossed. Never showing his face. Always keeping his head well below the rock face. With each successive *kaaa-thump* that vibrated roadside, he heard the whizzing of metal fragments sizzling through space. He heard the cries of surprise and the moans of agony as men met metal. He imagined the fragments tearing through the skin, smashing through arteries, slicing into organs, pulverizing bone.

Above the din, Traveler heard the sound of gunfire from behind him.

The second unit was riding to the rescue from the side of the road. A little too late, guys, Traveler thought, hurling the last nail bomb, hoping to seal the ambush.

He waited another few seconds until he heard the vicious thump of the *plastique*, then stood. Soldiers were tumbling and flailing all over the road. He opened fire with the HK, then jumped down from his vantage point, running for the door of the gun truck. He kept his HK91 at chest level, firing at anything that moved in his direction. The Glory Boys hadn't yet figured out the

156

direction of the attack, much less set up a counterattack. They were too busy dying.

He dove toward the driver's side of the truck, his heart pounding. He grabbed onto the handle and yanked open the portal. The driver fell out onto the roadway, his face a mass of ruptured flesh.

Nail grenade.

The man's partner was still alive . . . barely. The man had his hands upraised to his face. He was trying to catch his features. They ran through his fingers as he sobbed and screeched. Traveler leaned over, opened the passenger door, and shoved the man out. He slammed the door, hit the accelerator, and sent the truck slamming through the straggling convoy and down the road.

As the truck sped forward, the second wave of Glory Boys hit the road directly in front of him. Four jeeps and three dozen men on horseback appeared in the light of his high beams. Traveler cradled his rifle in one hand and grasped the steering wheel grimly as he prepared to ride the truck over the second unit. Much to his surprise, the Glory Boys scattered out of the way, allowing him safe passage. Of course, Traveler chuckled. These geeks thought that the truck was still being driven by one of their own.

Traveler almost doubled over with laughter as he sped past them. Only one man, on horseback, seemed to hesitate, seemed to question Traveler's authority. The cavalryman held his horse in check for a few seconds longer than any of the rest. The truck passed close by him. Traveler got a chance to eyeball the man, getting a good look at his face. The cavalryman got a chance to do the same.

Both men were surprised.

Traveler blinked at the headlight-illuminated spectre on his left.

It was Captain Peter Vallone . . . one of President

Frayling's most trusted military advisers, gung ho super patriot, a leader of men.

The man who had betrayed Traveler in El Hiagura.

In one, brief second, their eyes connected.

A hatred, which had smoldered for fifteen years, exploded.

"Vallone!" Traveler exclaimed, his lips forming the word that his brain refused to consider a reality.

Vallone reacted as if he had been shot. His entire body reared back atop the horse, watching his truck, his guns, and his assignment disappear.

Traveler caught the expression and laughed maniacally.

"Paxton!" the cavalryman cried. "I'll see you dead, Paxton."

Traveler gritted his teeth and stood on the gas pedal. He couldn't slow down. He certainly couldn't stop. Christ! How he'd love to just go back and slaughter that slime. But if he did that now, he'd lose the guns for sure.

He stole a glance at the chaos behind him in the rearview mirror. The second wave of Glory Boys was swarming all over the battle site. They were dazed. Confused. It would take them more than a few minutes to figure out what Vallone was bellowing about. In the meantime they'd search for the guerrilla in the rocks off the side of the road.

Traveler continued barreling toward the town. Knowing that Vallone was still alive enraged him but, in an odd way, enthralled him as well. He now had another reason for living.

Before he could die in peace, he had to track down and eradicate the traitorous bastard.

He smirked in the light given off by the bloodied dashboard. Yeah. It all made sense. If that spineless President survived the Big Bang, Vallone would have, too. Those two were inseparable.

Traveler spotted the town a few miles ahead of him. He stomped on the accelerator, sending the truck hurtling forward even faster. He figured that, by then, the army was on his ass. God knew who else was also en route.

He took a deep breath as the truck headed for the barricades. If Bess and Bellows had come through, Traveler would have a small but eager army waiting for him inside the city gates. If they had blown it, this nondescript burg might turn into his version of the Alamo.

# 26

As the truck carrying the guns plowed into the town's main street, Traveler beheld a sight that, to his way of thinking, bordered on the miraculous. Bess and Bellows, rifles in hand, stood in front of a group of ragamuffin warriors. The men's faces were pale and drawn, but there was a spark of life in their eyes that made the mercenary believe for the first time that they really had a chance of pulling this off.

Traveler pulled the truck up to and over a curb, grinding it to a halt with a screech of the brakes. As he clambered out, Bess waddled over to him.

"What took you so long?" she smirked.

Traveler stifled the urge to hug the immense woman. "I took the scenic route."

He trotted to the back of the vehicle. "Let's break out the rifles. I have a very angry group of Glory Boys on my ass."

Traveler cracked open a crate of heavy assault rifles while Bess struggled with a box of 7.62 NATO cartridges. "Give me that," Bellows muttered, rumbling up to the truck. "Women are so helpless sometimes."

He cracked open the box in one swift movement. The two men began distributing the weaponry to what passed for troops.

"What happened to Aikers and Milland?" Bellows asked.

Traveler tossed a rifle to an awaiting zombie. "They've killed each other off . . .I hope."

"Save the gory details until later." Bess chuckled. "I want something to savor over dinner."

"Sure as hell will be more appetizing than your food," Bellows grumbled.

"Arf, arf," Bess sneered.

"How many Glory Boys you have on your butt?" Bellows grunted.

"Enough," Traveler replied, "but we should be able to hold them off no sweat if these men can fire guns without screwing up."

"Don't sweat it, hotshot," one of the zombies hissed, snatching a rifle out of Traveler's hands. Traveler shrugged.

The rifles distributed, Traveler, Bess, and Bellows led their fifty zombies to the edge of the city. "The deal is," Traveler said while on the move, "that these boys are not going to expect your firepower. Let them get as close as possible to the city before you open up. We can take more of them out that way."

"Don't fire until you see the whites of their eyes, Cap'n?" Bess asked.

Traveler grunted and knelt down behind a wooden police barricade. He could barely make out headlights far down the road. "Here they come," he whispered.

The zombies crouched down behind abandoned cars, barricades, and debris.

"We have the advantage," Traveler advised in a soothing voice. "It's dark. We can see them, but they can't see us."

The Glory Boys came nearer. Traveler strained to catch a glimpse of Vallone. The darkness effectively obscured all facial features, however, so he had to make do with the fact that Vallone was indeed out there somewhere and, hopefully, a stray bullet would catch him between the eyes.

The jeeps and the mounted riders thundered toward

the town. Traveler turned and faced the zombies. "Take it easy, now. When I give the signal, fire."

The Glory Boys sped forward. They were five hundred yards away from the barricade. Four hundred.

"Easy," Traveler cautioned his men. "Hold on, tight."

Three hundred.

He could see the angry faces of the jeeps' drivers, illuminated by the headlights and the dashboards.

Two hundred.

The sound of hooves echoed throughout the empty main street of town.

One hundred.

"Come on, tough guys, a little bit closer," Traveler whispered.

The jeeps were only two hundred feet away from the town when Traveler bellowed "Now!"

He opened fire with his HK91, sending a spray of bullets across the first line of men. Two of the jeeps lost their headlights on that pass. A radiator began hissing. A cavalryman tumbled forward, horse and rider transforming themselves into crimson masses on the way down.

The townsmen opened fire as well; their aim was wild, but the amount of outgoing lead and steel was impressive. Traveler saw one of the men in a jeep stand up and make an overhanded motion.

"Everyone down!" Traveler yelled over the din.

An explosion rocked the street behind him. Grenades. He hadn't thought of that. He waited until the man made the same overhanded motion before he opened fire. The man with the grenade fragmented in the vehicle. The bomb dropped onto the backseat. The jeep, still hurtling toward the town, disappeared from the face of the earth with an enormous roar, a flash of blinding light, and a chorus of muted screams.

Traveler ducked as the air above him sizzled with flying fragments of hot metal. Getting to his feet, he

162

saw the wave of Glory Boys turn back and ride crazily down the highway.

"Are they retreating?" Bellows wondered aloud.

"Either that or regrouping," Traveler said. "Your boys here did pretty good for raw recruits. We hit those assholes pretty hard."

Traveler squinted into the night and scanned the blood-soaked ground outside the town. He didn't see any cadaver that remotely resembled Vallone. He attempted to hide his disappointment, but his irritation showed. Some of the ex-prisoners were chuckling and chatting openly, proud of their heroic stand against the invading Glory Boys.

Traveler spun around and faced the men. "Shut the fuck up!" he yelled suddenly. "Just shut up and listen for sounds. For movement. We beat them back once. Hooray for us. But we may have to do it again. And this time, they'll know just how to hit us. They'll know just where our strong points and weak points are. Point and shoot won't work again. Try aiming those pieces this time. You might even hit something."

Bess and Bellows remained silent. They exchanged a puzzled what's-eating-him look and walked away.

Traveler sighed and sat down on the ground. He was on edge again. The town around him was still. The quiet was broken by the distant crack-crack-crack of automatic weapon fire. The entire front line of defense listened as the snapping sound increased in frequency.

Traveler stood, stretched, and smiled. He faced the men. "Now you can congratulate yourselves. I have a feeling our Glory Boys won't be making a second pass."

The zombies whooped and danced, patting one another on the backs and chattering like chimpanzees. With amazing agility for a man his size, Bellows shinnied up a telephone pole and gazed off into the night. "Our Glory Boys just ran headfirst into some sort of patrol," he shouted down. "I can't tell if they're roadrats or what."

163

"It's whoever is left over from that wild-goose-chase war." Bess beamed.

"Yeah." Traveler nodded. "They'll be busy for a while, I suppose. Keep your men positioned at the barricades, and get some of them into the bunkers. You have enough guns and enough ammunition to hold off an invading army for quite a while. Who knows? If those idiots learn how to shoot those things decently, you might find yourself with a safe town here."

"My hero," Bess said, half-teasing.

"Yes, ma'am." Traveler sighed, fatigue hitting him like a wave. "Right now, I'm going to grab some shut-eye. I'll need a driver to take me out to my car tomorrow morning. Any problem?"

Bellows climbed down from the pole. "I'll take you myself."

Traveler shuffled back toward the hotel, leaving Bess and Bellows and the newly formed militia behind. "Hey, hero," Bess called. "How much do we owe you for all this?"

Traveler shrugged. "I'll sleep on it."

Traveler slogged into the hotel and paused in the lobby. He was hot. He was tired. He was thirsty. He had run an emotional gauntlet tonight and topped it all off by spotting the ghost of carnage past.

He needed a drink.

He walked into the dining room, pulled a bottle of tequila from behind the lunch counter, and sat down at a table. His hands were shaking. He couldn't figure out whether it was from exhilaration or exhaustion. Frankly, he didn't much care.

He poured a shot. Downed it. He was about to uncork another when he encountered his second major apparition of the evening. A bloodied, battered, and exceedingly irate Captain Zeke Aikers stood not three feet before him, aiming the barrel of a rifle quite neatly at the middle of Traveler's forehead.

Traveler decided to pour the second shot anyhow.

Aikers didn't seem to mind one way or the other. "You're dead meat, merce," he rasped. "I never should have trusted you. I never trust your kind."

Traveler drank the second glass down. He'd have to play this one by ear.

Aikers took no notice of Traveler's cool. He seemed quite determined to take the top of the mercenary's head off with his gun. "You hired killers have no sense of loyalty. No sense of patriotism. No sense of humanity. Do you realize how many men you killed tonight?"

Aikers was sweating. His hands were shaking. Traveler couldn't resist. "Oh, I don't know. Fifty? Sixty? A hundred?"

Aikers was not amused. In fact, he didn't even notice. He simply went on with his rant.

"And those men were a hell of a lot better than you'll ever be, scum," Aikers said, quaking with rage. "Now . . . before I send your brains splattering across the room, tell me one thing. Why did you do it? Why did you set me up?"

Traveler stared at the man soberly. "I don't know, Zeke. Probably for the same reason that I set Milland up and Moon up. . . ."

"Why? What did we ever do to you? We offered to pay you. We took you in. We gave you a cause to fight for."

"I guess that's it, Zeke," Traveler said wearily. "I'm tired of fighting for your causes. When I fight these days, I fight for people. You remember people, don't you, Zeke? They're those little, insignificant creatures that you brutalize, that you imprison, that you butcher to build an empire."

Traveler emitted a harsh, sarcastic laugh. "An empire. The three of you battling it out for *this* town? An empire? Do you realize how ordinary this town is? How bush-league? Yet you all dove after it like it was the Holy Grail. This stinking little hellhole was enough to change your stride into a swagger, your sense of order into bloodlust. You were a guardsman, Zeke. Yet you ran around here like a warlord. Man, you're no different than any other power freak I ever met. You, and guys like you, are into war. You get off on it. You like thinking about it, dreaming about it. It's mental masturbation, Zeke. . . . And like your mama used to tell you, too much of it makes you blind."

Aikers stared at Traveler for a moment, digesting the mercenary's monologue. Traveler made a move for the knife round his belt. Aikers casually fired a blast at the man, shattering the chair immediately to his right and smashing the tequila bottle into countless shimmering shards of glass and alcohol.

"The next blast you see will be your last," the sweating guardsman gloated.

He raised the rifle toward Traveler's head. Traveler swallowed hard. So this was it. Oh well, at least he succeeded in screwing up Aikers, Milland, Moon, and Vallone. Aikers would be cut down by Bess or Bellows as soon as he left the hotel, too. Although it didn't exactly please Traveler to know that he wouldn't live to see the town totally eradicate its two-legged vermin, he could at least die knowing that he had actually done something right for a change . . . with no strings attached, either. He had one or two more moves to make, but no real expectations.

He stared at Aikers's contorted face, realizing that it would probably be the last sight he'd ever see. Goddamn. That was a rotten thought. He had been hoping for something more romantic. A sunset, perhaps. Waves crashing against a deserted shore. Oh, well, there you go.

As he stared at the squat guardsman, a strange thing happened to Aikers. His face screwed itself into a portrait of outraged surprise. Something inside Aikers's head went crunch, and a small horn burst out from beneath his skull, protruding from a spot directly above his left eye.

166

For a moment Traveler thought he was hallucinating. Was Aikers some sort of were-unicorn? It wasn't until the slimy fellow began to tumble over that Traveler realized that the guardsman hadn't sprouted a horn but, rather, an arrow.

Twenty feet behind Aikers, the door to the small office ajar behind her, stood young Allison. In her hand was Traveler's crossbow. Traveler heaved a sigh. He had forgotten all about the girl and the weapon. Aikers's former victim slowly walked forward toward Traveler. She stepped over Aikers's body. She stood before Traveler. She handed him the crossbow, a confused look on her face.

"You have a great way of saying thank-you," Traveler said.

The woman nodded affirmatively.

"Sit down," Traveler said gently. He pulled up a chair next to his table. Allison lowered herself into it.

"Why don't you relax for a minute," Traveler advised, getting to his feet. "And I'll go get us something to drink."

He returned with a fresh bottle of tequila. He opened it and poured two shots.

"What will we drink to?" he asked rhetorically.

Allison shrugged.

"How about to marksmanship?" he queried.

The girl raised her glass. She spoke for the first time. Her words were delivered in a soft, halting manner. "That . . . was the first time I ever . . . fired . . . one of those."

Traveler didn't even want to consider that thought. He coughed gruffly. "Okay," he amended. "How about to dumb luck?"

The girl actually smiled. "To dumb luck."

They clinked glasses and drank down their toast. Traveler stood. He ran a hand through the girl's tousled hair. "See you later, kid."

He walked toward the lobby.

Allison stood next to the table. "Where are you going?"

"Upstairs," he called over his shoulder. "To get some sleep."

Exhausted, he avoided the stairs. He stood before the elevator. The door finally opened. He stepped inside the car. Allison trotted in just as the door was about to close. The girl gazed at the mercenary and smiled.

"What floor?" she asked.

Traveler blinked twice. "Uh, three."

"Three," Allison said as the car slowly began to rise. "One of my favorite numbers."

# 27

He lay on his back in the darkness. The black void beyond his eyes was a nightmare of ghostly visions which appeared and disappeared like faint flashbulbs. The room seemed too small for any human being to survive in. He was naked, his breathing strained. Her hands were slowly tracing the outline of his body, exploring every contour.

"You have so many scars," Allison murmured.

He couldn't answer. He couldn't tell her of the ones, the most important ones, that didn't show. His skin was on fire; pinpricks of heat welled up in every area her hand came in contact with. He could feel her long hair sweeping over his abdomen as she started to gently lick his stomach. His body shivered involuntarily.

"What's wrong?" she whispered.

He remained silent, staring at where the ceiling undoubtedly was. He gripped the sides of the small bed with his hands. Allison began to softly massage his chest. Gradually, he began to relax. Taking his left hand from the side of the bed, he began stroking her hair. He was surprised that the action struck him as perfectly natural.

He slid his hand through the blond strands. He had forgotten that some substances could be this soft, this sensuous to touch.

The flickering images of past insanity hovering before

him faded. Soon, only a mental portrait of Allison remained. His eyes gradually grew accustomed to the darkness. He gazed down at the woman. Allison was sprawled across the bed, the top half of her body suspended above his stomach. Her hands were outstretched. She continued caressing Traveler.

Something inside of him was changing.

He could feel it.

He wanted her as he had wanted no other for what seemed like several eternities. But he wanted her in more than just a physical way. Sex was easy. Sex was simple. Passion, however, was something else.

He suddenly wanted to tell her everything. He wanted to let her know that for years he had been just as crazy, as hard-assed, as gonzo as any of the goons who had ridden into this town. He had been as savage as any roadrat. As callous as any Glory Boy. He wanted to tell her that, in order to treasure the memories of a caring time, he had become uncaring.

But all that was changing, somehow. It wasn't that Traveler was becoming weak or soft or vulnerable. He had started a healing process.

Allison was part of it.

He wanted to tell her all that.

But he couldn't.

She peered up at him, surrounded by the thick folds of night, and gazed into his eyes. Traveler was taken aback. Allison smiled at him. She knew. She understood. She felt it, too. Perhaps, for her, this healing was also necessary.

He took her gently by the shoulders and pulled her up toward him. She straddled him gracefully, leaning forward, allowing him to tongue her breasts.

He lifted her into the air and raised himself to enter her. She inhaled sharply as he lowered her onto his scarred groin. He remained still, allowing her to rock herself back and forth slowly. Her rocking became more and more rhythmic, and after a time, he began undulat-

170

ing slowly in a counterrhythm. The speed of the move-ment increased. She began to moan in short, breathless bursts. The moaning became more and more sustained, intense. Traveler was dimly aware that someone in the room was matching Allison's wails. He was shocked to discover it was his own voice filling the room with emotion-charged grunts.

His head began to swim as the sound of Allison echoed in his ears. He felt every muscle in her body expand and contract. He smelled the sweetness of her sweat as it trickled down onto his chest.

She arched her back and emitted one prolonged cry as he exploded within her. She collapsed on him in a heap, her face pressed closely against his.

He remained silent.

He felt small trickles of moisture swim down the sides of his cheeks. Tears. But whose?

The two bodies in the bed hugged each other as if their lives depended on it.

Whose tears?

It didn't seem to matter.

# 28

Traveler sat in the dining room of Bess's hotel one last time, guzzling a brown fluid that Bess had assured him was coffee. Traveler wasn't quite sure if that was true. The stuff had a taste hovering somewhere between shoe polish and a cleaning solution he had once used to remove some purple paint from a brand new pair of blue jeans.

He placed the coffee cup down. Outside the building, Bellows and his men were loading the last of Traveler's "reward" into the Meat Wagon. Traveler had picked up a half dozen new rifles as a result of his stay in town, as well as a crate of ammunition and two tankfuls of gas—one poured directly into the van's tank, the other pumped into the portable bladder Traveler kept in the van's rear storage section.

Traveler smiled to himself. Why, Bess had even tossed in an extra knapsack filled with rations culled from her own private stock. Tasting the coffee, he wasn't sure if that was a plus or a minus.

As he drained the cup, he became aware of a pair of bright eyes peering his way from behind the lunch counter.

Traveler looked up as Allison walked from the counter to his table.

"You look very well rested . . . considering," she smiled.

"I don't need much sleep," he grunted, hiding his pleasure in seeing her.

Allison stared at Traveler. "I could come with you," she ventured.

The mercenary nodded. "You could. But what would you do?"

"I could fight."

"Uh-huh."

"I could help you."

"Uh-huh."

"I could . . ."

"You could get yourself killed," Traveler said without a smile. "Allison. You're a wonderful lady. I owe you my life and then some. I'd love to tell you that someday I'll pass this way again, like they do in all those old movies, but the odds are that I won't. You belong here, now. This town can be a home for you, now. The bad times are over. This place can prosper and grow . . . and you with it. You'll be safe here. With me . . . there's no telling what could happen."

He offered her something that passed for a grin. He extended a calloused, creased hand and caressed her cheek gently. He was surprised at the sensation he felt. There was no pain. No jingling of nerves. No flickerings of fear. There was just pleasure. Warmth. Affection.

The amazement must have shown on his face. He withdrew his hand as the girl began to laugh. Could it be he was growing civilized? He didn't want to think about it.

He stood up abruptly. "I have to go."

She remained seated as he strode out of the dining room toward the exit. "You take care of yourself," she called.

"I always do," he replied.

Outside, Bellows and Bess were in the midst of an animated conversation next to the Meat Wagon. An amazing change had occurred in Bellows during the last twenty-four hours; complacency had been replaced by courage, ennui by energy. Even Bess somehow seemed more kinetic.

Traveler glanced around the town. The cars left over from the Army-Milland-Aikers-Roadrat skirmish had been retrieved and were being repaired. The recently released prisoner-townsmen patrolled the city boundaries with brand new weaponry. It looked as if the town would finally begin running itself properly.

A few of the stores that had been boarded up were already opened. Ashen-faced citizens Traveler had never seen before scurried about inside. The mercenary wondered just where these people had hidden themselves for the past few years.

Bellows saw Traveler approaching. "Lazarus," he said, "you're all loaded up. You have enough gas and supplies to take you anywhere you'd like for the next week or so, first class. . . . Although knowing your supernatural ways, you could probably run this car and stay alive through sheer willpower."

"I just may try that sometime," Traveler said, opening the door to the driver's side of the van and sliding inside.

"Are you sure you can't stay?" Bess asked, leaning over the door.

"Positive."

"Where will you go?"

"I don't know. Somewhere."

Bess backed up from the car and put her hands on her massive hips. "Well, my Traveler, how does it feel to finally be a bona fide hero?"

Traveler colored at the remark. "I'm no hero, Bess. I'm just a man with something to do."

"And what is it you have to do, hero?"

Traveler stared at the vast expanse of burnt-out land sprawled outside the town. "I have to find four men."

"For what?"

"To cure three and kill one."

Bess burst into a hearty laugh. "You see? You *are*

174

getting noble, buster. Three out of four votes for life is a pretty good average for a mercenary killer."

Traveler nodded, offering her a lopsided grin. "Well, there you go."

He started up the Meat Wagon and gave the two-some one final wave. He accelerated the car. As he drove out of town, he glanced in the rearview mirror. He felt a wave of warmth spread slowly through his body. He couldn't understand its presence, exactly. The town looked just the same as it did when he had driven in a few days ago.

He kept his eye on the rearview mirror as the Meat Wagon sped away from the city toward the rising sun. Vultures fed on the remains of a dozen slaughtered roadrats on the side of the highway. What the birds of prey didn't snatch the wild dogs did. Traveler missed it all, his attention focused on the mirror. There was something about that last view of the town that mesmerized him.

Finally, he noticed it. There were people on the streets. Men. Women. Even a few children.

The Meat Wagon headed into unknown territory, with Traveler watching the image of the townspeople fade in the rearview mirror. It was an image he didn't want to let go.

It was just how the world used to be.

It was just how he remembered it.

The Meat Wagon swerved to avoid a pack of wild dogs.

Traveler glanced in the mirror one last time. Maybe, just maybe, the whole world would look that way again someday.

He held that thought as the sun bathed his face in its fierce, white glow.